BENEATH THE BOG

BENEATH THE BOG

D.Z. HOLLOW
JULIET ROSE

ABOVE THE RAIN COLLECTIVE

First Printing February 2026

ISBN: 979-8-9933717-2-6

Cover by Juliet Rose, D.Z. Hollow

Cover photo by D.Z. Hollow

Editing by Juliet Rose

Formatting by D.Z. Hollow, Juliet Rose

abovetheraincollective.com

Contents

To our Irish grandfathers, James and Robert

PROLOGUE

THE BOG BROODED A dark presence, much like the forest surrounding it. A thick patch of moss hung from the grassy knoll as trees twisted their way through gnarled terrain. Murky and opaque, with a thin, slimy sheen of algae on the surface, the bog encompassed a thatching of exquisite hardwoods. This particular stretch of greenery, although enchanting, hid a terrifying underbelly. Amongst the beauty, a dithering light, an ember of hope flickered in the shadows. The woods lay silent as something evil rustled in the leaves.

Caught between the limbs and scraggly underbrush, a spirit as ancient as the forest itself stirred. Something had drawn it to the surface: a desire, a want.

Hovering in the shadows, she observed the small boy, waiting patiently, her intention journeying deep below the roots nestled at her feet. Barefoot, she hiked toward the child, who'd wandered from his family's property. Oblivious to the young girl eyeing him from afar, the small lad admired the scenery before noticing glaring eyes watching him.

She moved closer, wanting to touch the soft flesh of the child, unlike her own rough skin. He seemed so pure and at ease in his surroundings, unaware of the danger stirring nearby. His naivety only made her want to capture him more. Make him her pet, her human toy.

Snatching the toddler, the dark spirit fled, dragging the child across the forest floor toward the mucky water. Rocks dug into the little one's tender flesh, scarring his back as the being took him far from home. Kidnapped, the boy became a part of a sinister breed of creatures dwelling beneath the bog. The poor child kicked and screamed as the hands of evil yanked his appendages, clawing at him as he cried out for a mother he'd never see again. Like that, the boy vanished out of sight.

Neighbors searched far and wide, even dredging the bog. All they ever found of the child was one lone shoe on the edge of the clearing.

Chapter 1

"Goddamnit!" Brennan slammed his hand down on the end table next to the answering machine. He plopped down on the couch and ran his hand through his curly, red hair. "Fuck Carson."

Marly came to the living room door, her face twisted in concern. "Everything okay?"

Brennan glanced at her, setting his face into a more acceptable state. He smiled at Marly, even though he didn't want to. "Just more bullshit with my brother."

She came over and sat down beside him, placing her hand against his back. "What did Carson do now?"

"It's not bad enough we recently buried our grandfather, and our grandmother is being moved to memory care, now Carson thinks we should take a last-minute trip to Ireland to 'discover our roots'. Everything to him is a game. A stupid, fucking game he expects us all to play."

Marly chewed her lip and spoke carefully, knowing Brennan's anger could surge in a split second. "You aren't considering it, right? I mean with-"

"Fuck, Marly, do you seriously think I would? Is that how little you think of me?" His words were biting, and she involuntarily flinched. Brennan immediately felt bad for his response and took her hand in his. "Sorry. I wouldn't leave you to go traipsing off to another country. We need to figure out what we are doing with, well, you know."

It was hard to even say. When Marly told him she was pregnant, it was the last thing he was expecting. They were in their late-twenties and had been dating since their last year of college, however, they'd only recently moved in together. They'd talked about marriage, but as a general idea, not a set plan. Abortion was out of the question with their Catholic families. Even moving in together had caused an uproar from both sides.

So here they were. Not married, a baby on the way, and Brennan wasn't even sure he wanted to stick around in life. Suicide crossed his mind every day. He couldn't explain it, but nothing made him happy. Not even fucking. Nothing.

On the other hand, his twin brother Carson lived as if he were high as a kite every moment of the day. He walked around with a perpetual half-assed grin and a plethora of full-assed ideas. Growing up, Brennan was always the one to get them out of trouble with his calm demeanor, while Carson was moving on to the next idiotic idea.

Marly rose and stretched her back. She was only a few months along, but a small bulge appeared on her normally too-thin physique. Brennan couldn't explain why, but it seemed alien to him to see it. He didn't feel a connection to what was growing inside her. Not even when he heard the heartbeat for the first time.

She reached down and placed her hand on his cheek. "I love you, Bren."

He smiled and touched her hand. "I love you, too, Marly."

He did. That wasn't the problem. He loved her with the abilities he had, but he wasn't sure that was what other people felt. He wasn't sure that's what she felt. Her love seemed so much more full, more encompassing. His love felt like a thin wire connecting them. Important, but not free.

Marly glanced back as she went to the kitchen, her hazel eyes concerned for him. "Maybe call him back. You know Carson. He'll probably be onto a new idea within an hour, anyway. You want anything from the kitchen?"

Brennan shook his head. "No, thanks."

After she left, he stared at the phone for a minute, considering whether he should call back or let it blow over. As he reached out for the phone, it rang, and he jerked his hand back. No, it wouldn't be Carson again. His brother wasn't that persistent. It was probably their father. He'd been calling regularly since their grandfather died.

Their family relationship was complicated. Their mother had died in childbirth, giving birth to their baby sister, who also passed. Their father was good to the confused, four-year-old twin boys, but distant. He seemed more concerned with his own mother than with his dead wife and baby daughter. The twins gravitated to their grandfather, who'd become their main caretaker in the aftermath.

Now, he was dead. Brennan touched the phone as it continued its shrill alarm and clicked it on. "Hello?"

"Brennan, it's your father. You have time to talk?"

"Sure, Dad, what's up?"

"I am taking your grandmother to the facility today. Are you meeting me there?"

Brennan really didn't want to. His grandmother was a harsh woman. It wasn't unlikely that she'd lash out at the boys as they grew up. Find some perceived misbehavior to focus on, always seeming to be mildly disturbed by their presence. She adored their father and barely tolerated their mother. She almost seemed relieved when their mother died.

"Yeah, alright. What time?" Brennan replied in his usual measured way.

"Be there at two-thirty. We will have dinner with her at the facility and speak to her doctors once she is settled in," his father answered distractedly in his clipped tones. "Tell Carson, as well."

Brennan wanted to tell his father that Carson wouldn't come. That twin didn't feel the obligatory guilt of being the perfect son like Brennan did. That was Brennan's burden to bear alone. He stared up at the family picture on the mantle. Back when he and Carson were little, and his parents were happy. His mother's green eyes flashed in the picture, and her smile showed nothing more than a woman content with her life. His father, however, seemed to stare right through the camera lens into another world.

Brennan looked like their mother but was more reserved like their father. Carson looked like their father with almost black hair and dark brown eyes, but was more like Brennan remembered their mother to be. Always laughing and planning fun adventures. No one believed they were brothers when they were kids, much less twins.

"Alright, Dad. I need to go. I'll let Carson know if I can get a hold of him. See you later."

"Only family, you understand?" his father ordered.

"Yeah, I know." He hung up before his father could say anything else. The guilt trips were monumental. Marly wasn't family in their minds. Their grandfather had liked her, but he was gone and could no longer run interference.

Brennan thought about calling Carson, but then he'd get stuck in a conversation about going to Ireland. He wasn't ready for another fight. He'd tell his father he couldn't get Carson on the phone when he showed up at the facility.

The familiar twist in his stomach started, and he stood up, grabbing his wallet and keys. If he had to face his grandmother and father, he needed to find something to eat to settle his gut. Marly was cooking in the kitchen, bacon and eggs, it smelled like. Now that morning sickness had passed, she was eating everything in sight. He didn't fault her, but it wasn't what he wanted. His body craved something else.

He slipped out without saying a word to her. She'd want to go along, but he needed to do this alone. Besides, his father had made it clear she wasn't welcome. He closed the apartment door quietly and padded down the stairs, his sneakers moving silently. As he pushed open the door of the building to the outside, the sun blinded him, and he raised his hand to shield his eyes from the glare. Providence's weather was unpredictable, and the warm front they were in was unusual for March.

He skirted through the city streets, knowing exactly where he was heading. When he arrived in the district of town, people like him rarely went to, he scanned for what he was looking for.

There she was.

A tall, fake-blond woman with large ruby lips and false eyelashes. Her short skirt was too snug for her round rear, so parts of her spilled out.

She saw him and smiled, lipstick smearing her teeth. "Hey, my little, red-headed freak. You back for more?"

Brennan dropped his eyes and peered around. No one was paying them any mind. "Can I, um... Desiree?"

"Aw, honey, you know I always have some for you. Come on, then." She meandered toward a back alley, her stiletto boots clacking on the sidewalk.

Brennan followed like a hungry dog, desperate for what she had to offer. She opened a faded and peeling blue door and glanced back with a wink before ascending a set of rickety stairs. He stayed right behind her, his appetite growing. The closer they got to the top, the more his heart raced in his chest. He needed this.

Inside the dingy apartment that smelled like perfume and sex, Desiree took off her faux fur jacket and watched him. "The usual?"

"Yes, please," he murmured, kneeling on the floor. Desiree walked around him, a sly smile on her lips. "You sure that's all you want? You know you can fuck me in the ass, right? I love being fucked in the ass."

Brennan dropped his eyes. She always did this. Tried to get him to do other things. He only had one thing on his mind, though. The one thing that made him feel alive. "No, Miss Desiree. Just the usual."

She sighed and leaned close to him, her chest brushing his face. "Damn. Too bad. I bet you have a beautiful cock in those jeans. Alright, grovel."

Grovel he did. Brennan pressed his forehead against the sticky linoleum floor, his arms stretched out before him. "I am garbage. I am nothing. I am worthless. I should be cut into pieces and disposed of like trash."

Desiree laughed, her voice like a tinkling bell. "I don't believe you."

Brennan knew he needed to dig deep to get what he desired. He lifted his head and licked her boots. "I am scum, slime at the bottom of rotting meat. I am a festering boil, human waste. Please, Desiree... I need it."

She sighed and crouched down before him, her genitals just inches from his face. "Fine, garbage child."

She stood up and allowed him to rise. She handed him a bag and tipped her head. "Anytime you want more, you know where to find me. I'd like to work you over something fierce. Show you all my tricks."

He didn't meet her eyes but handed her a wad of bills. She took it, letting her fingers linger a little too long on his hand. She reached down and grasped his groin. "I'd even give you a free ride."

Brennan took a step back, not wanting to piss her off, but needing to get out of there. He'd never cheat on Marly. "Thank you, Miss Desiree. I am your humble servant."

She watched him as he scurried out, shutting the door behind him. He needed to find a place to be alone. He practically ran down the stairs and out into the daylight, then gazed around for a spot to find some solitude.

There was a small park with people shooting up and having sex out in the open, so he found a secluded corner, ripping open the bag. As usual, Desiree provided. Inside were toenail clippings, pubic hair, a bloody tampon, a small bottle of liquid, and shit smeared on a napkin.

Brennan immediately began to suck the tampon, his dick growing hard. He disposed of the tampon once he could no longer taste the blood. He began to stroke himself and shoved the nail clippings and pubic hairs in his mouth, swishing them around.

He washed them down with the vial of urine, then licked the shitty napkin until he came hard into his hand. He consumed the hot semen and closed his eyes, satisfied. For the moment. The urges never stayed away for long.

A few minutes later, he strolled out of the park and tossed the bag into the trash can as he straightened his clothes. He swished his mouth out with a travel-sized bottle of mouthwash and set his face into the one the world found acceptable.

Chapter 2

"Stupid Brennan. He's so Goddamn closed off all the time. He's been that way since birth," I complained, smashing the payphone receiver down, causing a stir in the bar. I wasn't angry, but upset.

Life felt meaningless. I'd tried recently to make the best of it, see things for what they truly are, but my brother was a wall with a tiny crack in it. Nothing comes in, but a little seeps out, until the whole thing breaks like a busted dam. The walls could collapse, and still, it wouldn't matter to him. He'd still be shut off internally. That's exactly how I see my twin, Brennan. The firstborn son, by only a few minutes, of course, but he's a goddamn know-it-all.

Fuck him and fuck our dad.

He wasn't the worst pops, but he wasn't great either. After mom died, where was he? We needed him the moment the air hit our lungs. The second we were released from the womb, we had no choice; we needed our father. All newborns do.

Where'd he fuck off to?

A broken shell of a human, barely a vessel, merely a person—an eviscerated cartridge removed of all soul and life force, that's all he is to me. At least, that's what I've told myself over the years. "Dad is a piece of shit," I grumbled, taking a swig of my vodka tonic. Ordering another double from the handsome, young bartender, I winked, finishing my drink.

"You sure? You're tying one on tonight, huh, Carson?" he said to me.

"Yep. Now get me my double, sailor boy. Yeah, you're something alright," I slurred, trying to be charming. "Cute, but not my type," I whispered under my breath, my mind undressing him, nonetheless.

I needed to let loose, and this shithole dive bar wasn't the place for that kind of thing. With drab walls and drab men, it wasn't my scene, but they let the drugs flow and turned a blind eye to most underground things.

Wielding an eight ball of cocaine and a wad of cash, I hoped to get wild that night. Either a man or a woman to fuck, preferably both at the same time. I've always swung both ways, ever since high school.

Whatever got me high, whatever got me off.

The bartender smiled as he handed me my watered-down booze. "You alright there?" he asked, placing a napkin on the sticky, damp woodgrain of the worn top.

"I'm fine. I'd be better if you were naked," I replied with a grin. "I'm only kidding. Let me settle up and piss out of here," I added, throwing a twenty on the counter. Retrieving a cigarette from my jeans, I downed my drink, catching my bracelet on the fringe of the denim.

"Fucking prick," the bartender joked, handing me my change as his fingers lingered on mine an extra second.

"Night, man," I said, stumbling off the stool, giving a half-hearted wave back. I went to fish for a cigarette, but realized I already had the one I'd snagged seconds before in my mouth, waiting to be lit. With a shrug, I patted my pocket for my lighter and chuckled. "You're fucked up for sure."

"Night, Carson," the bartender said as he focused on another patron.

"G'night," I replied, sauntering out of the bar. "If it's one thing I love about Rhode Island, it's the sailors, the loose women, the boats, and the salty seas," I stated, grateful for the cash in my pocket.

I build ships and work the moors for a living. It's hard money, but I'm around good-looking guys, and the ladies love it—it builds up your muscles, too. It's good pay, providing funds for almost unlimited booze and drugs—the important things in life.

Walking away from the pub, I lit my cigarette, spotting a nightclub a few blocks away. Cars splashed through inky puddles, rock music beating from the passing vehicles. The city thumped, fully alive, much like me.

A group of teens drove by, and one yelled, "Eat a dick, mister!" Laughing, I wandered beneath the streetlights and city bridge, maneuvering past the park, darting across the concrete.

The Anchor was an eclectic dance club on the edge of downtown with strong drinks and guys looking to have a good time. A prominent fuck palace with beautiful women, a real haven for all the degenerates in town. It was my go-to when I was drunk and horny. Bright, neon lights lit the establishment, giving it a unified glow of fluorescent pink and purple.

As I slugged across the pavement, I couldn't shake how distant my twin brother, Brennan, had become lately. It was like he didn't understand how much family meant to me. After everything we went through in our childhood, he was the most important thing in the world to me. He didn't reciprocate, though, treating me as an afterthought. Ever since he met Marly, he hasn't been the same. Nights alone and bad breakups seemed to be the norm for him until Marly came along. Now he acts like he's more important than me, more adult, even.

Brennan's an odd one, for sure. I mean, there's always been something off about him. He seems like two people trapped under the same skin, fighting to get to the surface. I can't quite put my finger on it, but it's there. Even as my twin, he was far out of reach.

I don't know.

Talking to myself, I wallowed, missing family and fighting sorrow.

"Ireland would be life-changing, it's what Grandpa would have wanted. It's what Mom would want, too," I convinced myself, waiting for the pedestrian crosswalk signal to flash.

Skirting the block, I smelled fried food and rich tobacco. I gazed at the moon, which hung like an illuminated orange in the sky, mocking me with each step. The ground glistened, and pigeons gathered on a electrical wire, huddled against the night. Leaping over giant puddles covering the crater-infested asphalt, I saw a bouncer friend of mine and smiled. He nodded with a grin, hopefully happy to see me.

"Hey, Carson, figured I'd catch you tonight. No charge, your entry is on the house," he whispered, letting me through the threshold as his fingers grazed my arm.

A haze of smoke filled the entrance way, and a group of girls argued in my ear, one screaming in the other's face, their words too pitchy to make out.

Packed and boisterous, the club blared, the sounds of Duran Duran's, *Save a Prayer*, booming from the house speakers. "Of course," I bitched, eyeing the bar and beelining for a liquor drink. "Duran Duran."

The band was a favorite of ours—a shared interest between brothers. It felt like a message. "Damnit, Brennan."

Growing up, music and movies were our life. We spent our childhood pretending to be our favorite band and going to the drive-in for horror flicks. We also loved traveling together, but even since Marly came into Brennan's life, we hadn't done so in years. I thought a trip to Ireland would not only help us uncover our heritage and connect to our Celtic roots, but also bring us closer together—Grandpa's death couldn't have come at a worse time. I've always felt alone and shut out by Brennan, by everyone, but now it's worse than ever. Now, with a kid on the way, I know he sees me as the loser brother who drinks too much, does drugs, and fucks everyone in town. I mean, it's true. I know I'm no saint, but hell, open up—be a sibling. Can't he see I'm hurting here? Be a brother, Brennan. I need you.

Grandpa was like a dad to us, and where the fuck is Brennan? Sitting at home getting bitched at by his pregnant girlfriend. They aren't even married, I thought to myself.

Approaching the bar, I ordered a shot of vodka and a beer. I pounded the liquor and picked up the brew, eyeing the men's bathroom. Wading through the crowd, I vanished into a nearby stall, slamming it shut behind me.

"Dumb Brennan. I know he's home. I bet he just let the answering machine pick up," I fussed to myself, pulling out my limp cock. I pissed then shook my junk a few times, realizing it wasn't ready for action. "Stupid drugs."

Putting my dick away, I pulled out my tiny makeup mirror with my other hand. I sat on the toilet with my pants at my ankles, taking a shit. I used my razor blade to carve a few chunky lines. Snorting a fat hunk of coke, the burn penetrated my nostrils. It felt good when it hit my brain, however.

"That's the shit," I said, leaning back and letting my dopamine levels skyrocket. "Oh, yeah."

Snorting another chunker, I rubbed my nose violently, shook my head, and immediately tasted the incessant drip. The pleasant numbness set in as I swallowed the snot working down my throat.

"I'm calling his ass later when I'm super fucked up at four in the morning. That will really piss Marly off," I chuckled, putting the mirror, baggie, and faded bill back into my pocket.

Stepping out of the bathroom into the nightclub, the crowd grew rowdy. A groovy baseline thumped through my chest as I felt the low vibrations of the dance song in my core. A tight snare drum pulsated in my drug-infested brain as the narcotic took hold.

I felt raw and alive—my energy infectious, everyone wanting a piece of me. Shoving my way onto the dance floor, I sang along to the chorus. "How does it feel to treat me like you do?" The music pumped through my soul, turning me on.

I felt orgasmic, needing to find a release soon. Chugging a *Miller Lite*, I headed to the bar for a whiskey and another ale, the bartender looking me up and down. "You look fucked up, Carson. What are you up to tonight?"

"I'm going to Ireland to get in touch with my roots tomorrow. My grandpa died. He was like a father to me, and Brennan, he's off in all hee haw land or whatever baby shit that is, that fuckin' Old Mickey Deez shit."

"Old McDonald?" the bartender snickered, pouring two pints of beer.

"Never heard of him," I joked, pulling a cigarette from my acid-washed jeans. Laughing, I walked away, heading outside to smoke on the patio, noticing a couple making out, a guy and a girl. They were deep into it, groping each other with horny, drunk eyes. The guy had his hand down the chick's pants, rubbing her pussy with vigor. I watched, feeling like a creepy pervert.

After a while, they saw me touching myself, and the next thing I knew, I was at their place sucking and fucking the rest of the night away.

"DAMN IT, WHAT DID you get into?" I said, rolling over on the stained mattress. Looking around, I heard someone stirring in another room. Turning to my left, I saw no one beside me. Still, regret consumed me. Records hung on the wall, alongside pictures of nude men and women. The stereo played quietly, a t-shirt slung atop it. An ashtray sat on the bedside stand, crammed full of butts beside it.

"Shit," I groaned, my head buzzing as the room spun around me.

Locating my underwear, pants, and shirt, I high-tailed it out of the apartment with a brutal hangover. I moaned, crossing the street in search for a payphone. Traces of sunlight poked through the trees, as birds released their gentle choir. It would have been beautiful if I didn't feel like death from the prior night's debauchery.

Spotting a phone beside a pizzeria, I rushed across the road and picked up the black receiver, shoving a quarter in the rusty slot. Everyone around me shuffled, lost in their own charade. Buildings, although filled with people and things, seemed empty to me. The whole town felt lost.

"Maybe it's me," I said, hearing thunder crack, as rain fell all around me. The power lines drooped, littered with crows and morning birds, adding to the dawn chorus. I waited and waited as the phone rang and rang. *Fucking, Brennan.*

Frustrated, I hung up, slid the returned quarter through the slot, and dialed again. Still, it rang and rang. I waited, and after some time, the answering machine picked up. Sighing, I unraveled.

"Brennan, it's your brother, you know, your twin brother? We were in the womb together and shit. Anyway, I tried calling you last night, and the day before, and the day before that, but haven't heard a fucking peep from you. If you don't want to go to Ireland, fine. Fuck you. I'll go without you. Your loss. Have fun with Marly since she's all that seems to matter to you at all anymore. Peace, brother," I slurred as I hung up, realizing my brain may still be drunk from the previous night's bender. "Screw him."

The town looked grey and miserable as the rain subsided, much like my mood. Climbing into a taxi, I headed to the airport with just the clothes on my back, my passport, and a fat stack of cheddar.

Going to Ireland required me to fly to Logan Airport in Boston first. After a few hours' layover, I'd cross the pond and make my way to meet my ancestors, upset that my brother was such a fool. Lying to cover the wound, I told myself I didn't want him to go, anyway.

"Who needs you, Brennan? Certainly not me."

Chapter 3

The memory care facility smelled like a mixture of sanitizer and something else Brennan couldn't quite place. Almost like someone's home, but no one he'd ever known. He walked up to the front desk, feeling like an intruder.

"Uh, Deirdre O'Leary?" he asked the tired, middle-aged woman sitting behind the counter.

She barely glanced up and pointed to a sign-in sheet. "ID. Sign in and take a seat."

Brennan dug his driver's license out of his wallet, handing it to her, then scribbled his name on the sign-in sheet along with the current time. It was well after four in the afternoon, making him over an hour and a half late from when he'd agreed to be there. He'd gone back to the apartment after his morning excursion and listened to the messages on the machine from Carson again. Marly had left for work, so he took time to figure out what he was going to do about his wayward brother.

There were multiple messages and even more missed calls from Carson. It was obvious to Brennan that his twin was dealing with their grandfather's death much like the way he dealt with everything else. Getting obliterated and hooking up with whoever would let him.

Brennan didn't care that Carson ping-ponged between men and women, sometimes both at the same time. He did worry Carson would get himself into a situation he couldn't get out of. Carson never listened to Brennan, anyway, so he quit trying to reason with his unruly brother.

However, this idea to jump on a plane to Ireland was even out there for Carson. Where would he go? Did he have a place to stay? Brennan felt a familiar ache behind his eye and sighed. According to his last message, Carson was heading for the airport. Brennan hoped it was a threat, and Carson was home, sleeping it off. Calls to Carson's number went unanswered.

This brought Brennan to his other pressing issue. Meeting his father and grandmother at her new home. The memory care facility. Unfortunately, the home she and his grandfather had lived in Brennan's whole life had been reverse-mortgaged and snatched up by the bank as soon as his grandfather died. His father was paying for memory care. Why they'd reverse-mortgaged the house, he didn't understand. Unless to make sure the boys never saw a dime of inheritance.

They had been well off. Not his grandparents when they first arrived in America, but his grandfather worked hard as an electrician until he moved up and was able to buy a house. Good investments led to a fairly comfortable life. The boys' father and mother continued that cycle, and they never went without. At least, for their physical needs.

Emotionally was another story.

"Brennan O'Leary?" a voice snapped him out of his thoughts. He glanced up to see a young nurse holding his ID and a clipboard.

"Here," he said and rose. She smiled kindly at him, but with the disinterest of someone who couldn't afford to get attached in her line of work.

She handed him his ID and a badge to wear. "Put this on where it can be seen at all times. This will let guards know you can go in and out. If you aren't wearing it, you won't be able to enter or leave, so leave it on."

"Guards?" Brennan asked, confused. He was thinking his grandmother was going to a nursing home, not a prison.

The nurse nodded and gestured with her head to the front door. "Sometimes they make a break for it."

They, being the residents. Brennan frowned. "They aren't allowed to leave?"

"Not on their own. In memory care, we run the risk of them leaving and forgetting where they are, even who they are. We take them out daily, though, so don't worry about that. We want them to have the best life possible here, despite their conditions."

That made sense. His grandmother didn't even know who he was half the time. The nurse walked down the hall and paused for a guard to unlock the door to let them through to the memory care wing. Brennan suddenly felt like a small child and questioned coming here alone.

The nurse paused at a door and knocked lightly. "Deirdre, your grandson is here to visit you."

No sound came from the room, and Brennan considered leaving. Maybe she was asleep. That's when his father came to the door, an angry expression lacing his face. He waved the nurse away and glared at Brennan.

"It's about time you showed up! Can't even make time for your ailing grandmother. Where's Carson?"

Brennan felt his face get hot and shook his head. "I don't know, Dad. I tried calling him a few times, but he didn't answer."

"Sounds about right. You two don't care about anyone but yourselves. Come on, then. Your grandmother has been waiting." His father stormed back into the room.

Brennan followed like an admonished child, his head low. The room was strange. Not quite a hospital room, not quite a home. Some of his grandmother's belongings were placed haphazardly around the room, like someone had made an effort to designate the space as hers. However, it gave off grade school vibes and seemed out of place.

His grandmother was sitting in the bed, her thin legs covered by a white sheet and an afghan she'd made some years before. Brennan glanced around for a place to sit and settled into a wooden rocking chair near the bed.

"Hi, Grandma. Are you settling in to your new home?"

She stared at him for a moment like she didn't know who he was, then sighed as recognition crossed her face. "This isn't my home. Why are you here?"

Brennan glanced at his father, who was staring at his grandmother with puppy-dog eyes. His father reached out and took his mother's hand and squeezed it. "Mama, I asked Brennan and Carson to come visit you."

"Where's Carson?" she asked in an accusing manner.

They both stared at Brennan like he was his brother's keeper. Brennan wished he could curl into a tiny ball and disappear. "Sorry, he couldn't make it today. Maybe tomorrow," he lied.

His father looked away, disgusted, but Brennan's grandmother eyed him, not believing a word he said. She peered at her son. "I'm hungry, Colin. Go get me some food to eat. Who knows when they will feed me in here."

"Mama-" he started, but she glared at him, stopping him in his tracks. He obeyed like a child, rather than the fifty-something-year-old man he was.

Their relationship always embarrassed Brennan. His father was the only child born to his grandparents, and when his father was around his grandmother, he became a sniveling, weak toddler. His grandfather often chided Colin to toughen up and be his own man, but something about Deirdre's presence prevented Colin from being his own person. Thus, he took his frustrations out on his twin sons.

After his father left the room, Brennan glanced around, wondering how long it would be until his grandmother completely lost her mind. She'd always been off, but lately she'd taken a rapid decline out of reality.

As if she sensed his thoughts, she leaned forward and laughed bitterly. "You'd be so lucky, boy. You have no idea who I am or where I come from."

Her words were odd, but he chalked it up to the dementia. "I know who you are, Grandma. You came from Ireland with Grandpa when you were both in your twenties to start a new life. Then, you had my father."

She narrowed her eyes, something flickering behind them. "I never would have come here if it wasn't for..."

She stopped there, and Brennan tipped his head. "To America? I thought you came for a better opportunity?"

"They would never let us be. They would have dragged me back under and made me kill him."

Kill who? Brennan stared at his grandmother, who seemed to be deep in a memory. Likely slipping out of lucidity. It was as if she didn't know he was there anymore.

All of a sudden, her eyes became clear, and she met his eyes. "They will kill Carson for vengeance. For your grandpa taking me away."

"What?" Brennan was trying to make sense of her words. He knew better than to read into them with her dementia, but she seemed so insistent.

"If his foot touches Irish soil, they will find him and take him under. What is theirs' is always theirs'."

Did she know Carson was planning to go to Ireland? His hands began to sweat. "Grandma, have you spoken to Carson? Did he tell you something?"

Her eyes gazed up at the ceiling like she was seeing something he couldn't. She began to laugh maniacally and pointed up. "One-way ticket. That's what it is. There's no coming back. Carson is gone. Gone, gone, gone. Liquid and bone, never come home."

Brennan felt the hair rise on his arms and had a desperate need to leave the room. To call Carson. They had their issues, but now he was worried about his brother. His grandmother had been slipping mentally for some time, but her words scared the hell out of him. What the fuck did *liquid and bone, never come home*, even mean?

Brennan got up and stepped into the hall, willing his nerves to settle. A memory surfaced, and he allowed it to gel. It was when he was around nine or ten years old. Their grandfather had taken Carson and him to the beach. Carson was playing in the waves as Brennan built a sandcastle, and their grandfather was watching Carson, his brow knitted. Brennan had asked if everything was all right.

"Did I ever tell you what happened when I was a boy?" his grandfather replied.

Brennan shook his head. "No, what happened?"

"They found me one day, no memory, no family. Your grandmother's family took me in. At least, that's what they tell me. I don't remember much from when I was little. Doctors said I had amnesia. Your grandmother and I ran away when I was, I guess, around fourteen and she was seventeen. We lived on the streets. She said her family didn't like me anymore, but they had taken me in. My memories of them faded; I never really understood what happened. But I loved her, and that's all that mattered."

Even then, Brennan felt like it didn't make sense. His grandfather never seemed to have a clear picture of his childhood. Only that Deirdre was always there and took care of things. Once they lived on the streets, then later came to America, his memories were solid. Before then, it was as if he were reciting a story of someone else's life. The only consistent part being Deirdre.

Once the family tree got past Deirdre and his grandfather, it ceased to exist. With that and the death of their mother and baby sister, Brennan couldn't fault Carson for wanting to find their roots. Brennan didn't have that drive, but he had Marly. Carson had no one. Except for a brother who didn't give him the time of day. Brennan felt genuinely ashamed. He'd let Carson down.

Now, with their grandfather gone and their grandmother on the verge of not knowing who they were, it became more apparent that Carson's need to make sense of it all. To understand where they came from, where they belonged. Who they even were.

Liquid and bone, never come home.

Those words repeated in Brennan's head, and an overwhelming wave of terror ran through him. Carson wasn't coming home.

Not on his own.

Chapter 4

I flew into Logan International Airport with a three-hour layover. It was a long time to wait until my next flight, but I needed it. I'm not a huge fan of flying; in fact, I hate it. However, a load of booze and downers always does the trick. The extended time in the airport allowed me to drink, sleep, eat, shit, and call my dumbass brother again. The place was bombarded with people: kids, grandparents, drunks, and assholes loitering or rushing to their gates. It made my head hurt just being there.

I sulked across the airport, searching for a bar to get a liquor drink. I despised paying airport prices, but didn't have much of a choice, considering. With it close to nine in the morning, I didn't care how I looked, drinking alcohol in the packed airport. Not that anyone seemed to notice, anyway, caught in their own busy realities.

I ordered a cocktail and consumed it in one continuous swallow. The noise of the terminal, with the hustle and bustle of fellow travelers, exhausted me. The blaring overhead communication with relay of flight departures and delays overwhelmed my thoughts, so I ordered another double vodka drink and sucked it down before heading to the smoke lounge. In there, I sat amongst the tobacco haze. Tourists prepared for their journeys in every direction.

Thankfully, I found the lounge quiet, but it reeked of pipe tobacco and clove cigarettes. A guy yelled at his girlfriend on the phone, making everyone around him uncomfortable. He looked like he needed an ass-whooping.

I wondered if anyone else was going to Ireland like me. I saw a guy in a red sweatshirt, puffing a chubby cigar, staring me down like a cop or some shit. I almost said something to him, but decided against it, ashing my smoke before heading out. My buzz had me feeling warm and heavily sedated as I walked to my gate to find a bench to sleep on until my flight boarded.

After an hour and a half, I woke up, and it was time to get on the plane. I eyed a payphone and wandered over, shoving a quarter inside the slot, trying to reach Brennan one last time. It rang and rang until I gave up.

"No answer, of course."

Frustrated, I boarded, smelling of booze and stale cigarettes. The plane was full of all kinds of folks preparing for international travel. There were so many children and old people, the whole plane smelled like farts, but the flight attendants were polite. A sexy couple seated nearby nabbed my eye, and my thoughts drifted to them naked.

A stewardess smiled as she helped an elderly lady into her seat beside me. I liked her skirt and wondered if I could join the Mile-High Club on this flight. If I were lucky, maybe I'd get to do it twice. The thought made me chuckle, and the lady next to me grimaced, shifting away from me.

The pilots boarded, tipping their hats to an attractive, blond flight attendant. She smiled, and both men smiled back at her as if they had a secret between the three of them. A toddler a few seats up hit his dad with a stuffed animal as his mother sighed. Somewhere, a baby wailed in the back, creeping into my tired mind.

"It's going to be a long flight," I bitched, rubbing my head.

I hated life as I settled into my seat. I put the pillow behind my head and reached for my yellow cassette player and headphones. Pulling out the few tapes I brought with me, I settled on a mixtape of Depeche Mode, Talking Heads, and Joy Division. Industrial sounds pulsated against my eardrums, the arpeggiated synths and chorus blocking out the crying baby. I knew it would be a miserable trip across the ocean, so music and liquor became my vice, as always—my true soulmates.

A young girl behind me kicked my seat, the thrusting of her foot against my back enraging me. I wanted to scream at her and smash her oblivious parents' heads in, but I pushed the anger down deep inside as my father taught me, then headed to the bathroom to do my last few bumps of coke before take-off.

The techno music throbbing between my ears buried the chaos in bass and drum machines. Visions of darkness filled with sexual fantasies surfaced. I slipped into the tiny bathroom, smelling and seeing the blue dye sanitizer in the steel toilet, the basin incrusted with vomit on the inside.

"Guess, I'm not the only one partying," I said, quickly sprinkling my last line onto my makeup mirror and ripping the drug, pinching my nose as it burned. Shaking my head, I coughed and leaned back.

"That's the good shit," I muttered, immediately feeling the high bombarding my brain, my serotonin receptors exploding as I entered a state of bliss.

In thirty minutes, it would end, and I'd want a cigarette. "Fuck it, smoke one in here," I convinced myself.

Kicking on the fan, I lit my Marlboro, sucking it down like my vodka at the airport bar. The smoke filled the small space, drawing into the fan with ease. I knew it smelled, but I didn't give a damn who knew, the nicotine aiding the cocaine coursing through my veins. Sneaking out of the bathroom with a head full of nose clams and reeking of the Marlboro man, I cackled, feeling like a child stealing cookies.

"It's all part of the thrill," I whispered.

As I took my seat, the same guy in the red sweatshirt eyed me. I didn't like it, but I pushed the paranoia aside and removed my headphones. The pilot came on and let us know when we'd be arriving in Dublin. I didn't listen to what he said; instead, I put my tunes on and let my cassette play until the little bit of coke wore off, and I passed out.

At first, my dreams were placid. I saw Brennan and me as kids. We were playing in the woods behind our grandparents' house. The trees swayed as the sun shone through the fluffy clouds, ferns, and moss decorating the greenwood. Crickets and birds chirped as we walked toward a pond.

All of a sudden, I felt something pull me underground. Roots and decay devoured me, then swamp water rushed in. Toads, insects, fish, and bog debris filled my lungs.

I WOKE UP TO the pilot letting us know we were halfway across the Atlantic. In that moment, I began to feel uneasy. It's hard to explain—like a vortex strangling my chest. I suddenly felt sober. All the alcohol in me seeped out of my pores like vapor dissipating into the air. A dry vessel, I needed a drink, and I needed one fast.

Tremors overtook me, and the plane became claustrophobic—the pressure in the cabin growing too tight. Voices from the dark beckoned, and spirits filled the air around me. The plane closed in on me, and I felt my world shrink.

I wanted to bust a window open and jump to my death. That would bring sweet relief from this prison. A volatile energy passed through me, my fingers clenching the armrest.

The old lady beside me gave me strange looks as I twitched and screamed, "Let me off this fucking plane!"

I began convulsing, cursing, and foaming as my eyes turned red. Something kept feeding off me. I could feel it as I tore at my skin, trying to get free. The hag next to me alerted a flight attendant, and the next thing I knew, two men and a stewardess wrestled me to floor of the center aisle.

"He's on drugs!" a passenger in a U2 shirt yelled.

"Get the hell off me," I grumbled as the man in the red sweatshirt appeared, retrieving handcuffs from his pocket. He smiled as he cuffed me, his eyes glowing red like his hoodie. "What the fuck?" I screamed out loud, seeing his demonic gaze meet my eyes.

"See you soon," he muttered with a devilish grin.

I was bound and tied with a bungee cord for the remainder of the flight. My mind seethed. I felt separate from my body and a part of something dark and sinister. I heard voices, some male, others female, more unrecognizable. They sounded ancient and ancestral but demonic and ever-threatening. I struggled to make out the words amongst all the commotion.

Liquid and bone, never come home.

Floating in the aether, I could see myself on the plane as if I were outside my body, freaking out and flinging spit on myself. Part here, part there. There and nowhere at the same time.

"He smells like a distillery," a passenger stated as they put a pillowcase lightly over my head to try and calm me down.

Eventually, I drifted to sleep, dreaming terrifying nightmares of being burned alive.

When we landed, they freed me from my shackles and hurried me off the plane without anyone saying a word. Shoved into the crowds of the airport without so much as a second glance, I found the nearest pub.

Chapter 5

Brennan could feel the emotional heat coming off Marly as she stood across the room with her arms folded over her chest. Marly wasn't a yeller, although sometimes he wished she would. Just to get it out there in the open and hash it out. No, she let it fester, and it came out after hours, or even days, of unending steam. Granted, Brennan played the game of acting stupid and confused, which only set her off more.

"Hon, I don't know why you are upset with me. Carson is my brother. You say family is important, and he is my family," Brennan bargained, keeping his eyes wide with innocence, even though that was the last thing he felt. He was working her over, and they both knew it.

Marly crossed the room and plopped down on the couch. "Don't give me that shit, Bren. You know damn well you are springing this on me last minute. Carson made an idiotic decision to board a plane to Ireland without thinking. Without considering anything. Do you understand what is going on over there? It's not safe."

"Marly, that shit is going on in Northern Ireland. Carson went to West Ireland in the Wicklow Mountains, where our family is from. It's not the same place. It will be fine."

"I thought you didn't talk to him since he left. How do you know where he went?" Marly asked, her voice laced with accusation.

While he hadn't talked to Carson, his brother had been leaving messages on Brennan's answering machine as he made his way to Ireland and to the county their grandfather said he was from. At least, he could give Carson credit for that. When Brennan stopped hearing from Carson, that was when he needed to get worried.

"He went where our family lived in Ireland before they came to America."

Marly eyed him, attempting to read his face for a lie. "So, do you think it's a good idea to follow him over there? Did you even think to ask if I wanted to go along with you?"

He hadn't, and now he could see he'd fucked up. "I didn't think you'd want to go, being pregnant and all. Do you even have a passport?"

"No, but that's not the point, Brennan. You could've at least asked me! We are family, too, you know?" she spat.

Tears sprang to her eyes, and Brennan could see she was hurt by his actions. Rightfully so, he was being selfish.

"Babe, I'm sorry. I wasn't thinking. I was so worried about Carson, I wasn't thinking straight. He's so damn irresponsible, and I'm afraid he'll get himself in serious trouble over there. You know how he is. I'm only going over to bring him back. Not for some fun vacation or anything like that. Do you want to go, then?" He really hoped she didn't. Dragging his pregnant girlfriend along sounded like pure misery for both of them.

She deflated and smiled. "Was that so hard? No, I can't miss work. Trying to save time for after the baby is born. Can you at least wait until after tomorrow? I have my four-month ultrasound, and we might be able to find out the sex of the baby then."

Brennan inwardly cringed. He wasn't ready to think of the thing growing inside her as a boy or a girl. It was easier when it was an abstract concept. He took her hand and smiled. "Sure. Speaking of sex..."

Her eyes darted away for a second, then, recognizing he was making an effort, she sighed. "Come on, boy, let's get you taken care of."

They proceeded to the bedroom and took their clothes off. Marly was beautiful with her long brown hair and big blue eyes, but the bulge in her lower midsection kept Brennan from getting hard. He pictured things she would be horrified if she knew about and felt the blood rush to his groin. Like a dog, the nastier, the better. He closed his eyes and imagined running his tongue around the inside of the toilet bowl after Marly used it, and his penis went into action. He wanted to stick his tongue up her ass and lick her clean, but she wasn't into that sort of thing. She wasn't a prude, but she had her limits.

She lay on the bed and batted her eyes at him. She'd read too many romance books and watched way too many rom-coms. He wanted to get dirty. He wanted her to shame him. Instead, he went over and climbed on top of her. She ran her hands down his back. He wanted her to claw him open. She drew him close in a delicate kiss, and he desired to taste blood. Even if it was his own.

Even so, he managed to get to completion, and she rolled over to fall asleep, whispering the kindest words he'd ever heard. Marly was like his mother. Gentle, thoughtful, caring. He didn't deserve that. He deserved to be kicked, to have filthy socks shoved down his throat, to eat from the bottom of the garbage can.

Once she was asleep, he crept to the bathroom, searching for something to satisfy the emptiness inside him. Her underwear was cast on the floor, but other than some discharge from her vagina on it, it had nothing. He sniffed it, but it didn't arouse him. The toilet was clean, too clean. Marly had been on a cleaning kick since the morning sickness abated, so there was nothing for him to get off on.

"Damnit," he muttered. The apartment was pristine.

Spying Marly's shoes discarded by the door, he picked them up and flipped them over. Nothing. She might be the tidiest person he'd ever met. What he really wanted was what a dog wanted. Human byproducts. Blood, excrement, hair, whatever pieces are so easily discarded as waste. It made him feel more human. Sometimes it was as if he was a creature in the skin of a man. He'd felt this way since he could remember. Only since puberty had it become sexual. Like a dog licking its own slimy, red penis, Brennan got off on the parts of himself he didn't connect to.

Just as he was about to stick a finger up his ass to see if he could fish out something to taste, he heard Marly get up and come toward the bathroom. He quickly acted like he was brushing his teeth as she slid past him to pee. Maybe she'd forget to flush.

She finished and hit the handle, sending the liquid swirling down the toilet. She came by and took his hand. "Come back to bed, I'm cold."

Brennan sighed and squeezed her hand, knowing he was out of options. "We can't have that."

He climbed into bed with her and wrapped his arms around her small frame. He loved her with every ounce of his being. He knew that and never doubted it. He hoped her love would be enough to stop his obsessions, his fetishes. He couldn't be like this when the baby came. Even if he wasn't keen on its arrival, he didn't want to be some freak his own child was ashamed of.

As he drifted off, Brennan saw the same image in his mind that he'd experienced since he was little, after his mother died. A face hovered over his. It started like his own image, then twisted into a horrid creature with long, pointed teeth in a large, creepy grin. Its breath smelled like shit, and blood dotted the end of each fang. The almond-shaped eyes stretched impossibly from end to end, and its angular chin practically touched Brennan's.

The thing was, Brennan was never afraid when it came. It didn't make him want to retreat under the covers or cry out. Instead, he often found himself reaching out to embrace the image, though his arms hit nothing but air. Even so, like a baby needing the comfort of its mother, the creature felt like home for him.

The next morning, the couple went to the ultrasound appointment like any other normal pair and smiled through all the doctor's questions and comments. As the wand moved through the jelly on Marly's abdomen, the doctor pointed out things about the baby growing inside.

Healthy, right on target. See, there's a foot? Oh, look, that's a hand waving. That's the spine and the heartbeat.

Then she paused and smiled. "Do you want to know the gender?"

Marly grinned at Brennan with excitement and nodded. He took her hand and was his best, dutiful boyfriend at the doctor's office. "Yes, please."

She moved the wand around some more, then pointed at the screen. "It's hard to tell, and it's really more about what we don't see than about what we do see. I can't say a hundred percent, but it sure looks like you are having a little girl!"

Marly gasped in delight and squeezed Brennan's hand. "A baby girl, Brennan! You don't have any girls in your family, right? This is the first?"

At that moment, Brennan's eyes rolled back in his head, and he hit the floor, convulsing violently.

Chapter 6

The wound inside me is ancient. It dates back to before my birth, before my time in the womb. It traces further down the rabbit hole than Brennan and me. All my life, I've felt punished for something that happened before being Carson O'Leary. I don't know what I did to deserve this agony, this wretchedness.

Am I cursed? I think so. Am I forsaken? Certainly. There is a reason my mother isn't here, and it runs deeper than human understanding. It digs below the surface, tearing away at the pieces of me that existed before this body. I hate this vessel, this contraption I'm in. It vexes my every last nerve. It pains my soul—my diminishing light. The dampening of my flame started from the birthing of my spirit.

My ancestors are Celtic. My roots intertwine with the soil of Ireland as I am an extension of eons of transformation and regret. Every bit of me is ready to give myself to the seed growing within.

To let it consume me wholly.

I don't need friends, and I honestly don't need family. Brennan is tethered to his own troubles and his own wickedness. I am free, an ever-unfurling frond of antiquity. My soul is lengthy, a tadpole with an elongated tail, dreading its forthcoming transformation.

Am I afraid of becoming like my father? Is this a self-talk of fear and concern? I don't know. I don't want to become like him.

DARK AND DREARY, THE pub was everything I wanted it to be, with its worn cobblestone floor and patrons few and far between. A couple of old farts sat at the bar, sipping a pint. Bleak atmosphere, beer with a creamy head, and walls weathered to the ceiling made the place feel like home. It smelled smoky and dank, and I asked for "one of those," like a tourist, catching a glare from a grey-haired man who shook his head as he poured the stout into a glass.

"Let the head sit," he groused, lighting a pipe.

I smiled and returned to my thoughts, my childhood memories plaguing me. With my brother betraying me and my grandfather gone, there was no one to accept me for who I am. All I want is to feel closer to him, closer to my heritage, to my family. I felt removed—empty, like the space between my brother and me.

Absent.

"You alright, lad?" the bartender asked, his gaze crooked like his nose and sly grin.

"Just got here from the States. My twin brother didn't want to come with me. Our grandfather died recently. He was practically a father to us. Happy to be here, though."

The bartender interrupted, his saggy earlobes hanging from his withering face. "Let me guess, your ancestors are from Ireland, yeah?"

I chuckled. "Of course."

"I see you boys all the time, so desperate to cling to your Irish roots. Look around, fella, Ireland is in turmoil. War waging everywhere, feckin' hell."

"I needed to get away. It's for the best. I'm here to discover things."

"Your heritage?" he asked, though his tired eyes told me he saw people like me all the time.

"Yeah, what else am I going to do? I feel like something is leading me here for a bigger purpose. There's something about my past I don't know," I admitted.

"Listen, I see you Americans coming over here, thinking it's better than there, the irony. As I said, be cautious. There are things here that will eat you alive. You seem like a good young fella, just be careful. Don't let your guard down too much while you are visiting."

"I'm here to drink booze, get laid, and discover my roots," I replied, sipping my Guinness and acting like an obnoxious American. Singing along with a Pogues song, my inebriation thickened with each pint. After four dry stouts, I moved to Irish whiskey, racking up quite a tab on my father's credit card bill.

I left the pub drunk as piss, fumbling with my matches and smokes, staggering with each footstep. I wandered down a back alley before scurrying around to a gift shop. Dublin reminded me of Boston. There were cars and people everywhere, so much chaos that it made my head swim, everything closing in around me.

I wanted to get out and see the countryside. I wanted to be where Druids thrived—to walk the labyrinth of Pagans and feel the earth in my bare feet. A part of my ancestry drove me forward. I could see the muck and mire between my toes as I met a green, mossy forest being swallowed by a beautiful bog in my mind's eye.

I wasn't sure why, but a steady current called me to the countryside. I needed to rent a car and escape the city.

Maneuvering through the shop, I bought a pair of sunglasses, a raincoat, some socks, stamps, a couple of candy bars, and a postcard to send to Brennan.

It read, *Wish You Were Here*, with a picture of an Irish castle. With the bag of shit in my hands, I hurried out of the store and spotted another pub to hit. The buzz from the previous place wore off fast. I wanted drugs and liquor. Maybe some sex, too.

Settling on a dive bar by a McDonald's I wasn't expecting to see in Dublin, I went in and ordered whiskey, and eyed anyone who might know where the cocaine was. I scribbled a note to my brother, simple and straightforward: *You should have come, you twat. I'll have fun without you because you fucking suck cock! - Carson*

I chugged liquor and asked the bartender if he knew of a mailbox nearby I could stick the postcard in. He mentioned one outside the pub, just a block away. I located the mailbox, tossing my letter to Brennan inside, snickering when I walked away. "What good is a twin brother if he won't come party in Ireland with you?"

When I went back into the bar, a beautiful redhead woman with porcelain skin sat beside my barstool. She hadn't been there when I stepped outside. I definitely wouldn't have missed her presence. She was gorgeous and provocative, and I wanted her naked, my mouth on her pussy. I could almost taste her sweet cum.

She turned and smiled, almost to say she'd been waiting for me all along. "Buy me a drink?" she whispered with an Irish accent.

"For you? Of course!"

The fire in her eyes matched her hair. I wondered if the carpet matched the drapes as she ran her fingers on my forearm. Her eyes were green like the trees, and the mole on her face brought me even closer to the earth.

"American?" she asked, lips reminiscent of fresh blood.

"Yep, guilty as charged," I laughed, praising my luck. "What are you having?"

"Whiskey, of course," she replied with a sly smile, so infectious it made my knees buckle.

The slight freckles on her shoulders and chest were visible beneath her black halter top. Curvy and well put together, with wide hips and nice legs, lust overtook me as I marveled at her beauty. She had ass and tits to boot. I could feel her luring me, hoping she wasn't a prostitute. I didn't have the funds for that.

"A whiskey for this beautiful lady," I ordered, motioning to the bartender.

He rolled his eyes and prepared the drink.

Enchanted, I introduced myself. "I haven't been in Ireland but a few hours, and I've already met the most gorgeous woman in all of Europe, lucky me. My name is Carson O'Leary."

"An Irishman, I knew it. I like the American-made Irish boys, not the typical slosh fest you see over here. You're different, easy to manhandle," she mentioned with a joking sneer. "My name's Brianna."

I wanted to fuck her right there in the pub for everyone to see, and hell, whoever wanted to join in.

We drank and flirted. I'd been with beautiful women before, but Brianna was exceptional. She had the skin of an angel and the hair of the devil—so fiery and explosive. Her curves were seductive, as were her thin, defined lips and chiseled cheekbones. She looked like a goddess, a pearl amongst a sea of garbage. I found the bar uninviting and repulsive, but here, before me, this beautiful being illuminated sex and lore.

I was sucked in by her eyes, her shape, and her voice. I wanted her, and I wanted her more than I ever wanted anything before in my life. "She's all that matters," I proclaimed. *A muse, a queen, a conductor.*

"I like your legs," I mentioned, running my fingertips over her creamy thighs, wanting to lick her flesh and spread her legs wide. I had to stop touching myself as we talked.

"Want to get out of here?" she asked.

All for it and ready to go, I fondled myself. "Yeah. I don't have a hotel or anything yet. I got off the plane hours ago. You got a place near here?"

"Sure, but let's get a room. It will be more fun that way."

"Let me guess, you're married, and you fuck tourists for fun? I'm into that."

"Something like that," she snickered.

Her smile lured me more. I wanted her mouth on my cock, I wanted mine on her thighs and chest. "I got a credit card, let's get a hotel room, and I'll fuck your brains out for the night," I told her.

"I like the sound of that," Brianna whispered in my ear as her fingers drifted across my crotch.

Tall, with long legs carved from perfect porcelain, everything about her screamed dominating and forceful. I knew sex with her would be incredible.

Paying the bartender, I kept my eyes on her ass as her skirt rode up, revealing her lacy black underwear, her glorious chest falling out of her top. I marveled at the size, wondering what her nipples looked like. I could practically taste them. No woman had ever made me feel this horny. I wasn't sure I'd even find a hotel, figuring most rooms were taken.

All I could think about was sex. Her sex.

We stepped out of the dive bar onto the crowded street, and I spotted a mediocre hotel a bit away. We walked across the street, the daylight peeking through the gray clouds. It wasn't even nighttime yet, and I was already shitfaced and ready to fuck the best piece of ass my eyes had ever seen.

We went in, and I paid for a room. Drab with maroon chairs beside a chipped table and a dim lamp, pictures of old people adorned the walls. Dust filled every corner, and cobwebs dangled from each threshold.

The attendant eyed me with disdain, and it dawned on me again, Brianna might be a whore. Honestly, I didn't care. I took another look at her and told myself, "No prostitute looks that good." Ideal in every way, I knew she craved me.

At least, that's what I told myself.

Entering the boring hotel room, a painting of a fisherman on a boat with storm clouds caught my attention, reminding me of the shipyard.

"Are you going to stare at the painting or my marvelous tits?" Brianna snarled as she dragged me toward the bed.

"I want a taste of those," I replied, caressing her ample breasts, running my fingers over her hard nipples. "You're perfect."

"That feels good," she moaned.

I pushed her onto the bed and continued kissing, while I removed her underwear—my tongue on her stomach, then between her legs, feeling the airiness of red pubic hair. As I tasted her, dark thoughts entered my brain. I suddenly felt detached from my body. I rose above the hotel room and could see myself below, face buried in Brianna's snatch, as she gripped my hair with her head tilted back in sheer ecstasy.

I saw her change, her face becoming demonic. Her mouth full of razor-sharp teeth, her eyes white like the moonlight. A strange, stringy, fibrous web sprouted from her vagina, reminding me of silicone, white with a yellow sheen. The material spread from between Brianna's legs and encased my head and neck, wrapping around me tightly like fishing line. I felt like vines were gripping

me, binding me inside this beautiful woman. A strong entanglement, I began to panic, screaming bloody murder. I returned to the moment, my face inches away from Brianna's sex.

"What the fuck is wrong with you? Haven't you ever eaten pussy before?" she said, shoving my head away in disgust.

Embarrassed and unsure of what had happened, I struggled to find the words. Creating sounds seemed difficult. At the moment, I became mute and transfixed, frozen in my shame.

"Fucking weirdo, these damn Americans," I heard her mumble as she put her skirt on and began dressing, covering up her miraculously barren body. I felt sick, my stomach bubbling with gas.

I ran to the bathroom to shit immensely, my belly aching like hell, gagging at the disgusting toilet covered in mildew and piss stains. The cracked mirror and stained towels seemed useless.

Peering in the toilet, I gasped. A purple caterpillar, about three inches long, sat in the bowl. Delicate and full of tiny, microscopic hairs, it glowed, squirming.

"What the fuck?"

I watched the thing fight in the bowl for a second before flushing it down the drain in fear. My rectum burned. I wasn't sure what to think.

Did that really just happen?

"Something about Brianna isn't right," I said to myself, wiping my asshole with toilet paper to check for blood. To my relief, there wasn't any, but a strange purple gunk dripped from my anus. It was putrid, smelling like an abscess, an opaque and foul substance.

What the fuck is happening to me?

Chapter 7

The sounds of machines beeping in a syncopated rhythm drew Brennan to the surface. He was caught in a spider's web and tried to move his arms to set himself free. His arms felt like lead, and his legs were pinned under a gossamer of spun silk, creating a delicate prison. He thrashed to break free and felt pain shoot throughout his head.

"Stop! You will hurt yourself," a voice to his left ordered.

Brennan forced his eyes open and was blinded by the sun. The spider came closer and leaned down, measuring its prey. Brennan squinted, his eyes refusing to focus.

The spider sighed and adjusted the webbing covering him. "See, now that's better. You gave us quite a scare," it said.

Us? There was more than one spider? Also, how did he scare *them* when he was trapped in their web? Brennan coughed past the pain in his throat. "Where am I?"

The spider stated something Brennan couldn't understand, and another voice came in. A familiar voice. He couldn't quite place it, but he'd heard it before.

"Brennan, it's Marly. You had a seizure. Well, seizures."

Brennan remembered something. Standing, staring at a screen, then everything went black. That was the last thing he recalled. His head was pounding. He tried to reach up to touch it, but the webs stopped him.

"No, don't do that. You have tubes in your arms for meds and fluids. Do you understand? You had surgery."

Brennan opened his eyes again, and they began adjusting to the space. The spider was only a man. The female, a pretty young woman with long, dark hair, looked familiar, and Brennan began to have memories. Marly, that was her name. She was his girlfriend. The man looked like a doctor. He was in a hospital room. Apparently, after the surgery he didn't remember.

"What happened?" he whispered, his voice crackling.

"You don't remember anything?" Marly asked. "About the ultrasound? The seizure?"

Brennan didn't know what she was talking about and shook his head. "My skull hurts."

"You had brain surgery," Marly explained. "After the seizure, something showed up on your brain scan. They went in to remove it."

"The good news is it isn't cancer," the doctor told him, not that cancer had even crossed Brennan's mind.

"What is it?" Brennan asked.

The doctor waved a clipboard and shrugged like they were talking about what to have for dinner. "We don't know yet. It's been sent to pathology for analysis."

Brennan stared at the doctor, who he now realized was a lot younger than he'd first thought. Maybe late thirties or early forties. The doctor pushed a pair of wire-rim glasses up on his nose and smiled at Marly. For some reason, this pissed Brennan off.

He cleared his throat. "Then, how do you know it's not cancer?"

The doctor redirected his focus to Brennan. "Well, we know what cancer looks like, and we have no idea what we pulled out of your brain."

"Can I speak to Marly alone?"

"Of course. Have the nurse page me when you are ready to talk more." The doctor slid the clipboard into a holder by the door and gave Brennan a brief wave as he left the room.

Marly came and sat in a chair next to the bed and took Brennan's hand in her own. They sat in silence for a few minutes, when Marly squeezed his hand and met his eyes.

"I was really scared. You were there, then the next moment, you were on the ground convulsing. They rushed you out of the room. I was still on the ultrasound table. The doctor helped me get up and dressed, but by then, you were taken away. I called your father, however, he said he couldn't leave his mother alone."

That didn't surprise Brennan. His father would always choose his own mother over his sons. Carson. Did he even know what happened? Or was he over in Ireland, having the time of his life while Brennan was fighting for his life?

"How long have I been here?"

"Four days."

"When can I leave?"

Marly glanced away, her eyes filling with tears. "I don't know. They are waiting for the results of what they removed from your brain. The lab here couldn't identify it, so they sent it out. It's better if you stay in here, where they can assist you."

He watched her for a moment, feeling the old abandonment seeping in. "Help me touch my head."

She frowned and began to protest, but could see he was going to manage it one way or another. She guided the tubes around him, so he could lift his hand to touch his scalp. His head was bandaged on one section, but he could feel they'd shaved his head bald. For some odd reason, that bothered him more than the idea of the surgery.

"Don't mess with it too much. You have staples in your head from the surgery," Marly insisted.

A wave of exhaustion came over Brennan, and he dropped his hand. He glanced around the room for his belongings, but they were nowhere to be seen. He was forced to stay there until he was released.

"Have you heard from Carson? Has he called?"

Marly dropped her eyes. "I think maybe he tried. The answering machine was blinking. I haven't been home for long. Just long enough to change clothes and shower. I've been here with you almost the whole time."

Brennan felt sick and looked around desperately for something to vomit into. Realizing what was happening, Marly grabbed a basin from under the bed and shoved it toward Brennan. He leaned over as the room spun around him and heaved into the plastic bucket. Not much came out except bile and saliva.

Marly rubbed his back, and he wished she would stop. His whole body felt like his nerves were exposed, and her fingers felt like razor blades being dragged across his skin. She pressed the button beside his bed, and a nurse came in, seeing his situation.

"I'll have the doctor up your pain meds and antiemetics next time he makes rounds."

"What?" Brennan croaked through an acidic throat.

"Meds that help you not feel so nauseous," the nurse answered as she switched out the basin for a clean one.

The nurse left, and Brennan lay back in the bed. He eyed Marly, seeing how tired she was. "I need to sleep. Can you go home and see if there are any messages from Carson? Maybe let my dad know how I am?"

She leaned in and kissed his forehead like he was a child. It felt nice, comforting. "Of course. Do you want anything from home?"

He shook his head, instantly regretting it. The room swam, and his eyes felt like they were vibrating in his skull. He attempted a smile at her, but his mouth wouldn't work. Marly gathered her belongings and paused, her face worried.

"Will you be alright while I'm gone?"

Her concern meant a lot to him. Especially considering no one else in his family gave a damn. He nodded. "I'm in good hands, right?"

She smiled. "Yes. I'll be back as soon as I can."

"Get some rest if you can. Don't rush back, you need to take it easy. For you and the baby," he whispered. The memory of the ultrasound came rushing back, and he stared at the bulge below her navel. The baby.

His daughter. His head began to throb again, and he winced. Marly took a step toward him, and he put his hand up to stop her. She froze mid-step and glanced at the call button. Brennan waved her away.

"I'm fine, Marly. Please see if Carson called. I'm really worried about him."

In an odd change of mood, Marly snorted. "Why? He abandoned you without two thoughts. Maybe it's time to think about yourself. You don't owe any of them your loyalty, Bren."

He didn't, but he couldn't help it. Family first had been drilled into his mind since he was little. He smiled at Marly with gratitude. She was only trying to protect him. "Thanks, Marly. Try and get some sleep."

She shook her head. "No, I'll be back as soon as I check on things at home and grab some stuff."

After she left, Brennan closed his eyes and willed sleep to come. Images of his mother crossed his mind, then were replaced with the image of the face he often saw when going to sleep. This time, it only watched him, its mouth closed in a grim line. Something had changed. He no longer felt the need to reach out to it.

When he opened his eyes again, Marly was back, reading in a chair. Brennan glanced at the clock on the wall and realized hours had passed. He didn't remember sleeping, but he didn't remember the time, either.

A light knock came at the door, and the doctor poked his head in. "Oh, good, you're awake. We got the results of your tests."

Brennan did his best to sit up, but his head wouldn't let him. The doctor came over and raised the bed slightly with a button. He sat down and opened the clipboard, frowning at what he was looking at.

"Have you traveled overseas in the last few years?" he asked, still looking down.

"No. I've never even left the United States," Brennan answered, confused.

"I see. Do you consume raw foods such as fish or pork? Anything exotic?"

Brennan blushed. Not food, but he definitely consumed things that might be considered exotic. Human things. "No. Can I inquire why you are asking these questions? What does this have to do with what was in my brain?"

The doctor glanced up, his eyes unblinking. "Well, what we found in your brain is, to be honest, quite strange. Similar to what they find in third-world countries or in people who consume uncooked animal foods. Very rare in this country, and not exactly what those conditions are. Yours is one of a kind."

Marly shifted in her seat, her eyes full of fear. "I don't understand what that means. What does the test say? What did you find?"

The doctor gazed between the two of them and stroked his chin. He peered back at the chart like it was going to tell him something different, then looked back up. He pulled his glasses off and clutched them in his hand as if they gave him strength.

"It seems you had a caterpillar growing in your brain."

Chapter 8

My anus throbbed, a deep pain radiating from inside my rectum. I could feel it in my stomach, my gut airy and spacious—similar to butterflies in my belly. Now I know where the saying comes from. Sitting on the toilet again, afraid to shit, I felt something slide out, and I hoped it was only feces.

Please...

It wasn't, rather it was a wad of glistening silk, delicate yet intimidating. Then, I saw blood and a sticky resin stuck to the sides of it.

What is wrong with me?

Scared and craving obliteration, my abdomen ached, causing me to feel nauseous. I coughed, feeling a strange string in my throat. The more I hacked, the more the thread caused me to gag on the fibrous thing caught in my esophagus.

Shoving my fingers as far down my throat as I could, I grabbed the thread and yanked, unraveling the string from deep inside me.

The vomit came next. Bile and saliva flung from my pale face as I hurled, pleading for the agony to stop. It was crippling, and I wanted to die. Once it subsided, I left the bathroom and saw Brianna was gone.

I darted out of the hotel room into the fresh air. Rushing to the nearest pub, I hurried across the street, clenching my stomach. An eerie mist rose from the pavement, adding to the ominous ambience and urban decay.

Ordering a double, I let the whisky pour down my gullet. It burned, but soothed the hurt stirring inside me. I continued to pound shot after shot until I felt plastered, stumbling out of the pub, almost crawling on all fours like an animal. I felt primal and sickly. I wanted drugs, and I wanted them now.

The city had narcotics. I was sure of it. Wandering down alleys, I eventually hit a nightclub. With it getting late, I knew the delinquents were emerging from the shadows. I couldn't remember how long I had been with Brianna or in the hotel room. Everything was a blur.

A mirage.

The club was everything I wanted it to be, but more. American dance halls couldn't hold a candle to the debauchery unfurling in the UK. Gritty and fluid, everyone partied, drank, and enjoyed themselves openly. The bass thumped, and the drums echoed like hail on a tin roof. The drinks were flowing, and the drugs were plentiful. I prowled, on the lookout for cocaine and cock. After my experience with Brianna, I had men on my mind... pussy being far from my thoughts.

I noticed a good-looking guy with golden-blond hair and sunglasses eyeing me. I couldn't look away, and he grinned. He came over smelling of Calvin Klein cologne and cheap booze.

"What are you looking for?" he asked, placing his firm grasp on my shoulder.

"Coke, weed, downers, whatever."

"I got it all. Weed, white, LSD."

"Let me take all three," I muttered over the dance music, holding out a wad of cash.

"Enjoy," he whispered as he took the money from my grasp. He handed me packets, then faded effortlessly into a mob of partygoers.

With urgency, I went to the nearest bathroom stall to drop the acid, snort white, and puff the Mary Jane. I swallowed the five hits of Lucy and carved out a line on my compact mirror. I could hear other people doing the same in the stalls beside me.

The cocaine felt good, rocketing through my nasal cavity on a mission, an exhilarating rush, causing me to rub my nostrils. The drip started, and I swallowed the leak, clearing out my sinuses. "That white bitch is good," I said, putting the narcotic away, reaching for my cannabis and rolling papers.

I was thankful I picked some up at the corner store. I planned to smoke hand-rolled cigarettes until I returned to the States. Lighting the joint, I puffed away, watching the haze billow around me.

Someone started beating on the bathroom stall, asking to hit the reefer. "Pass that shit," the drunk laughed, slurring and cursing up a storm. "Let me hit that fucker," the guy belted, banging on the frame.

"Get your own, man," I yelled back, blazing on the bone. "Fuck off."

"Oh, American, eh? I think I'm drunk. My name is Ian. Or should be, if I recall. Share one with a smashed fellow, won't ya', yeah? Look, I'm going to a party in the countryside, plenty of drugs and pretty girls. Share with me now, then come with me to the party?"

Enticed, I opened the stall door and handed him the half-smoked joint.

"What's your name, mate?" he asked.

"Carson."

"Where ya from in the States?"

"Rhode Island," I answered, irritated by the small talk.

"Oh, the small state, right?" Ian asked, wavering on his feet like he was being blown by the wind.

"Yeah."

"Whatcha doin' in Dublin?"

"My grandfather died—it doesn't matter," I mentioned, taking the shriveled joint from Ian's fingers.

We smoked and chatted before meeting up with two of his guy friends in the club. Climbing into a car for a ride out into the Irish countryside, I snorted a bump of powder. It was dark and hard to see, but the stars were bright, illuminating the heavens.

The LSD kicked in, and I felt strange and flimsy, my body limp and loose, like a worm. My skin seemed weird... sticky. I could feel something odd protruding from my belly button.

"Where are we going?" I asked, feeling uneasy.

"Wicklow Mountains, you'll love it."

"Wicklow, Wicklow," I muttered several times, enjoying the way it sounds. "Wicklow. That's where I'm going."

I must have been talking out loud because Ian and his friends laughed at me and my American accent.

"What are you on, mate?" Ian chuckled.

"I took some acid and cocaine."

"Going for it tonight," his friend joked.

"I'm in Ireland. My twin brother, Brennan, bailed on me. His girlfriend's pregnant, so he's probably getting off in her mouth right now. Fuckin' douchebag," I bitched, feeling the drugs take hold.

I felt like a jellyfish, oceanic and plasmatic. They were playing Tears for Fears on the radio, and I tried to remember what song, but the music dripped and pulsated.

Colors became sound, and rhythm, shades of purple and turquoise. I could feel a thread extending from my belly button—like an umbilical cord. It unfurled and unraveled, an energy encapsulated in my past.

I could feel a string leaving my anus and falling down my leg. Pulling it, I plucked the silk like a guitar string. It wobbled and vibrated. I wondered if Ian and his friends heard it, but they were too busy jamming out to the tunes pumping through the speakers. I saw the moonlight and felt obscure. The sight of the looming crater made me feel small and otherworldly. I didn't like that feeling.

The air shifted, light and ethereal as the constellations shimmered. My spirit wanted to fly, to greet the twilight and become one with the sky. It called to me, luring me home. Wherever that was.

The LSD worked its magic, and I was but a fly, an insect on the wall of time—not important, nothing but a caterpillar on the underside of a leaf. *Life can be minuscule. Life can be desolate. It can be lonely and brutal.*

Ready to disintegrate, I winced, the car ride becoming claustrophobic. My anxiety peaked.

What am I doing? I'm in a car with strangers in a country I have never been to before. Are these guys going to kill me? Do they know my secrets? Who was I before this life? Who am I now? Do I even know who I am anymore? I'm Carson O'Leary, a guy who's confused and out of fucking control. That's who I am. I'm like an electric eel.

My mind scattered and boomed thunderous thoughts, which turned into flavors. Songs smelled funny. I couldn't think straight. The lack of sleep, the bender of booze, the raging sex and drugs thrusted through me. I wanted to explode.

"Are we almost there?" I asked, my head jetting forward to greet the two strangers in the front.

"A few more minutes," Ian replied, turning up the music as he focused on the road. "Frankie says, relax."

I had no concept of what the song was, or even of music being played. The noise from the vehicle, the road, the windows rolled down, and the gentle night breeze made my flesh feel torn open. Something stirred in me, and it wasn't just the narcotics in my system; it was something much greater. The universe, the cosmos, the sun, the moon, the stars, and the sky were pushing me onward, further into the Irish countryside.

"That's my buddy Graham's house up on the hill," Ian commented, pointing to a well-lit home a few hundred feet ahead.

I couldn't take it anymore. I had to get out of the sedan. Ripping the doors open as the car still cruised, I jumped onto the dirt road. It hurt like hell when I hit the rocky ground, but I was thankful the car had slowed because of the rural road.

The vehicle stopped suddenly, and I heard Ian yell, "What the fuck, mate?"

My back ached, and my shoulder blades had a sensation like they were on fire. My skin felt like a moth being burned by the flame. I wanted to die, so I ran in circles, tearing at my body while the boys laughed at me.

In that moment, I yanked myself back into reality.

"Dude, you are fucking trippin'," Ian laughed.

He was right, I was. More than I ever had. I gathered my senses and followed the car as it slowly drove toward the house party.

"I gotta piss," I hollered, as they parked beside a van. A simplistic but well-sized house, there were about twelve cars out front. The house raged with people and loud music.

The ground spiraled and illuminated with hieroglyphic patterns and fractals. The acid now my master, and I its bitch. I pulled my pants down, admiring the constellations overhead, and a meteor passed by.

I chuckled, took my cock out, ready to pee on a tree, but something felt off. The tip of my penis was red and raw. It began to grow and shrink rapidly. It would become thin and elongated, similar to Pinocchio's nose, then it would shrink and look like a tiny pistachio. Mesmerized but terrified, I tried to piss again, but the urine wouldn't come out.

That's when I noticed the antenna coming out of my dickhole.

Chapter 9

"Come on, let me help you to bed," Marly coaxed, nudging Brennan's sleeping form on the couch.

The doctors had allowed him to come home as long as he had someone on hand twenty-four hours a day to keep an eye on him. That, unfortunately, meant Marly was his caretaker. Something that didn't sit right with Brennan.

It was his job to take care of her.

He rolled over and eyed her. "I can just sleep here."

She sighed and shook her head. "No, you can't. I'm supposed to be with you at all times. Where am I going to sleep if you sleep here? The floor?"

Brennan sat up and braced himself as the room began to spin. The doctors said follow-up scans were clear, but he would still have effects from the brain surgery for some time. Dizziness, confusion, things like that. They couldn't explain why he felt like he still had something growing inside his brain.

"Fine. You're right. Just give me a minute to settle myself. Go on, and I'll be there in a minute."

She watched him, unsure. "The doctor said-"

"I fucking know what the doctor said, Marly! I don't want to be treated like an invalid by my pregnant girlfriend. I need a goddamn minute!"

She flinched, and he immediately felt bad for speaking to her like that. Here she was pregnant with his child, having to wait hand and foot on him. It was embarrassing.

He shook his head and reached out for her. "Sorry."

Marly sat next to him on the couch, tears brimming in her eyes. "I know this is hard, Bren. I'm not trying to make you feel vulnerable. I only want you to be alright."

He smiled weakly. "I know. I'm sorry. Go on and brush your teeth, I'll be right behind you."

She rose and touched his cheek. He didn't deserve her; he knew that. She was like an emerald, and he was a dried-up turd. She clicked the hall light on and turned back to him with a wink. "I'm coming to check on you if you aren't there in five minutes."

He laughed. "Fair enough."

After she left, he picked up the phone and dialed his brother's number. It rang, unanswered. It was like Carson had hopped on a plane and simply vanished into thin air. He hadn't heard from Carson since he'd landed in Ireland

and said he was heading for the Wicklow mountains. Brennan hung up the phone and leaned back on the couch. He and Carson never had that twin telepathy he'd heard about from other twins.

Maybe because they were so different.

Even so, he closed his eyes and pictured his brother in his mind. All he could see was flashing lights and fragments of Carson, as if it were a film being sped up. He opened his eyes and rubbed his head. All he got out of that was that Carson was still alive. Probably getting fucked up somewhere.

As promised, Marly appeared back at the doorway and raised an eyebrow. She wouldn't go to bed without him, and he felt too guilty to leave her standing there. She already had a baby to take care of. He needed to suck it up.

He wobbled when he stood and watched as Marly stepped to help him. He put his finger up to stop her and grasped the edge of the couch. After a few seconds, the room settled, and he was able to walk over to her. She wrapped her arm around his waist in a sort of hug, really to make sure he didn't collapse on the way to the bedroom.

They stopped by the bathroom door, and Brennan smiled. "I got this. I promise. Just need to pee and brush my teeth. I'll be out in about a minute."

She let him go and stared as he shuffled into the bathroom. He could feel her eyes on him and shut the door as he made it inside. He needed some dignity. He brushed

his teeth and peered at the mirror. Growing up, no one believed he and Carson were brothers, much less twins, looking and acting so differently. Yet, when he gazed into his reflection, he could see Carson staring back.

Something was wrong.

Then again, Carson had a habit of putting himself in situations that were less than smart. If Brennan had a nickel for every time Carson did something stupid, he'd be a rich man. He dropped his eyes and glanced into the drain of the sink. He wondered if he could shrink down and crawl inside the tube. He would live there the rest of his life.

Marly cleared her throat, snapping him out of his thoughts, and he moved over to the toilet to pee. It took a minute to get it going, and the stream came out tinged pink. Brennan stared in confusion, wondering if the brain surgery could cause that. They didn't say anything about it, but the list of symptoms was a mile long, and he'd quit listening about halfway through.

He finished up and considered telling Marly, but then decided against it. She'd never let him be if he did. He flushed and figured if it was still that way in the morning, he'd decide what to do then.

Marly had the blanket pulled up to her chin when he slid into bed next to her. She smiled with her eyes closed and reached out for him. She was so beautiful, even in her pending slumber. Brennan put his arm over her and rested his chin against her head. She was the only thing not fucked up in his life. The only thing he had worth living for.

His mind went back to his mother. How much fun she'd been. She always had a game to play or a story to tell. Their father was distant at best, but their mother was all in. Carson and Brennan were everything to her. Then they found out about the baby. She was so excited about their sister. Though, the twins didn't know it was a girl until after their mother and the baby both died.

Brennan began to doze off and felt Marly roll over the other direction. She'd told him he made her hot since she was pregnant. He let his arm drop from around her and rested on his back, his mind between being cognizant and dreaming. Images floated around and became his dreams once his mind quit fighting sleep.

He could see his father in the dream. He was watching as their mother coaxed the boys to sleep. Their dad was frowning and leaning on the door jamb, telling her to hurry up, not to coddle them. When she stood up, it was clear she was extremely pregnant and kissed each of the boys on the head.

She moved out of the room, pausing at the door to look back at her sons. She rubbed her belly as she did so, all of her children within arm's reach. Their father sighed and shut the door behind her as they stepped out of the boys' room.

Where the dream should have ended, Brennan instead was seeing his parents from that night. His mother was walking down the hall, then grabbed her stomach as liquid ran down her legs. She nodded at their father, who rushed down the hall to make a phone call.

When he came back, their mother was on their bed, grimacing with the contractions. Brennan didn't know this part, but they never left for the hospital. His mother cried out as the waves of pain began to come fast and heavy. Something was very wrong. No doctors or nurses were coming.

Who had his father called?

As time sped up in the dream, Brennan saw his grandmother arrive. She had a bag with her and went to their mother's side. Again, the time increased in speed, and the baby made its way into the world. A girl!

What should have been a glorious event quickly became a nightmare. As their mother watched helplessly, Brennan's grandmother took the baby and smothered it to death with a blanket. Their mother cried out, trying to get to her daughter to save her, when their father stepped forward at his mother's request and put a pillow over his wife's face until she stopped breathing. Both mother and child, murdered at the hands of those she most trusted.

Brennan jerked awake, the horror of the dream washing over him. Had his father killed his mother? Had his grandmother killed his sister? Why? It couldn't be real, only his mind making things up because he was thinking about his mother before he fell asleep.

Marly was pregnant, and his injured brain was simply worrying about her and the baby. It all made sense if he thought about it that way. Losing his mother in childbirth, finding out he was having a daughter. Carson going missing. Even his grandfather's death and his grandmother being put in a home. Stress had simply taken its toll on him over the last few weeks and caused him to have nightmares.

Or so he thought.

Until he realized he was standing over Marly as she slept, curled up in her blanket. Brennan shook his head and felt the weight of something in his grasp. His eyes followed down the length of his arm to his hand and what he was clutching for dear life.

A knife.

Pressed to the belly of the woman he loved and the daughter she carried.

Chapter 10

"What the fuck?" I muttered, watching the head of the caterpillar protrude from my throbbing peehole. A surge of electricity rocketing through my extremities caused me to panic. For a moment, the drugs stopped, and my mind cleared. I could see the tree in front of me, breathing and becoming a psychedelic menagerie of intricate proportions.

Looking down at my cock, I saw nothing. There wasn't a bug or creature coming out of my genitals, so I took a deep breath and finished pissing. Then, I listened to Ian laugh, telling Graham about the dumb ass American they found huffing drugs in a bathroom stall in town.

The party bumped, and I craved some dick, hoping there were no insect-looking mother fuckers in the house, cause I'd bug out, pun intended.

I shook my junk and tugged my pants up. The sky mesmerized me as I gazed up at the constellations, admiring the swirling cosmic hues. The acid attacked in full force, yet I still felt as horny as a rabbit. I needed to fuck, and I was going to find my mark.

As I approached the abode, Ian introduced me to Graham. He had dark hair and a thick, bushy beard, and held a liquor bottle in his hand. He wasn't my type, too Grizzly Adams for Carson's taste. I wanted a clean-cut, fit man with a big hog, and by God, I'd find him.

"Nice to meet you, Carson. There's another American lad around here. His name is Jeffrey, and he's from Michigan. The big fella with the sideburns over there," Graham mentioned, pointing to a chubby guy in an Echo and the Bunnymen shirt.

"We probably know each other," I joked with a bruting, sarcastic tone.

I walked past Graham and Ian, into the sea of folks getting pissed on beer and liquor. I could smell reefer and sex stirring and wanted in. I headed into the house. A thick, smoky haze lingered over discarded plastic cups.

"Fucking Duran Duran," I bitched, hearing the sounds of yet another song Brennan and I loved.

That fucker is probably sucking his own dick, fucking perv. I don't need him, anyway.

My mind unraveled as I shoved the memories aside, the music a reminder of the abandonment. We'd had enough of it with losing Mom, and Dad's bullshit. Now, my twin was being selfish and self-centered, as well.

"What else is new?" I whispered, making my way through the crowd of unruly Irish partiers.

I immediately started looking for the backrooms, opening closet doors and pantries until I found the degenerates—the drug-snorting kinfolks. There were two of them hiding out in a back bathroom, so I knocked on the door and told them I had cocaine. The door on the wood frame flung open, and there stood two men, who introduced themselves as David and Flynn. Flynn was enticing, pale, and muscular. He screamed Rugby player and huge cock. David, on the other hand, was gangly with glasses and curly hair. Cute, but nowhere near what I was on the hunt for.

The bathroom looked enormous, and the walls shrank, growing rapidly in my drug-induced haze.

"Who the hell are you, mate?" Flynn asked.

Flashing the powder and stepping in, shutting the door behind me, I snickered. "My name's Carson," I said, dumping cocaine on the mirror on the counter.

"An American, then? Welcome to the other side."

"Nice to meet you both. I just kinda ended up all the way out here from Dublin. I caught a ride out here with Ian, you know him?"

"Yeah, Ian's cool, but can be a bit of a prick," David snickered.

"He never has drugs, but always wants in," Flynn laughed in agreement.

"That's how we met, smoking pot in the bathroom at the club, and he forced his way into the stall."

"Typical Ian," Flynn said softly, giving me the *come fuck me* eyes.

"Here, do a bump," I commented before ripping a massive line of white, letting the powder do its thing, as I realized I might lose my shit. The room vibrated, the headrush astounding. I worried I might faint and split my skull open on the disgusting toilet seat, so I sat on the counter.

"Oh boy," I said, watching Flynn snort his. "Aren't you something," I admitted. "I could fuck your brains out."

Wasting no time, I started kissing him, feeling under his shirt, and touching his nipples. I didn't care if David was his boyfriend; Flynn would be mine tonight.

It became clear David didn't swing that way, but Flynn certainly did. Flynn was squatty but rock hard, despite the narcotic pumping through his veins. Feeling his erection through his shorts, I then slid my hand in, rubbing his sex. David slipped out, leaving us alone, which was fine by me.

My hand stroked Flynn's penis. "Quite the bulge. I'm impressed," I whispered, noticing him harden more.

Taking him in my mouth, I struggled with the girth. I wasn't used to a man like Flynn, but that was okay.

Everything suddenly shifted, and I watched his penis shrivel and die in my hand, screaming as I ran out of the bathroom. Embarrassed, I went outside to smoke.

Muttering to myself, I took drag after drag. "What just happened?"

Flynn followed me out. "You alright?"

"I'm sorry. It's the drugs, too much coke and 'sid."

"You look fucked up, your pupils are insanely dilated," Flynn pointed out.

"I'm so fucked up and dealing with a lot of shit. My grandfather died recently, he was from Ireland. I have a twin brother, and, well, he's a piece of shit. He didn't want to come, so here I am. Broken and lost. My life is a mess. I feel unsure about who I am or where I come from. I don't know why I'm unleashing to you. You don't know me."

"I just had my cock in your mouth, mate."

"True," I chuckled, puffing my cigarette.

Flynn looked at me, his face swirling with illumination. Soft and tender, he reminded me of my mother. Shaking my head, I felt energy swelling inside me. The memory triggered another wave of emotions, and I began to weep.

Flynn comforted me, being soothing and nurturing, something I wasn't accustomed to. Not since my mom died. I wanted to feel uncomfortable, but I didn't.

"Look, mate, you need to be careful, especially out here in the Irish countryside. There are things here that are evil. They live in the forests, and they take and take. They feed off the weak and vulnerable. I can tell your heart is heavy, and your intentions are pure, but you're clouded by a shroud of darkness. It's like an evil spell, I can see it coming off you. My family is ancient, my line is deep. I know the spirits around the greenwood are mischievous and seductive. Be careful tonight," Flynn warned with extreme caution.

I wanted to laugh, but he'd shown me such care, I couldn't. "I'll be fine, bud," I told him, placing my hand on his shoulder.

I struggled to make sense of everything, the acid taking the lead now. I could hear Flynn trying to talk to me, but the visuals were getting intense. My childhood flashed before my eyes, and, all of a sudden, I left Ireland.

Back in the States, I was only three years old, with my mother and Brennan at the beach in Newport. A sunny sky filled with giant, puffy clouds hung overhead, and I could feel the coarse sand between my toes. My mother glowed with radiance, a beaming ball of comfort. Her smile enveloped my tiny core as I wiggled my fingers and watched seagulls in the breeze. I could smell the sea and salt all around me. The waves moved in and out gently, creating a soothing rhythm. I was content in the perfection of the moment.

Not a care in the world.

In that moment, everything shifted. I was back home with my mother.

“Mother,” I uttered, keeping my gaze on her young face. She appeared so youthful and full of life, a dandelion in a green field, the lone beacon. She turned my face to hers, her eyes worried.

“My son, please leave this place now.”

CHAPTER 11

BRENNAN FOUND HIMSELF IN the street, still wearing his boxers and bathrobe. After waking to find he was holding a knife to Marly's belly, he'd dropped the blade and ran. Well, tried to run. His body and brain still weren't in sync, and he moved in a disjointed, haphazard way. Miraculously, Marly didn't stir from her slumber, and for that he was grateful. No sane part of him wanted to hurt her or the baby. He couldn't bear to see her wake up afraid of him.

He paused in an alley and leaned against the damp brick wall, reflecting on the dream that led up to the horrible awakening. His father and grandmother had killed his mother and baby sister. *In the dream,* he reminded himself. Not really.

Right?

He shook his head, not being able to erase the vision of his mother desperately trying to save her daughter and herself. It wasn't real. It couldn't be. His father was detached, but he loved their mother. At least, as far as Brennan could recall from his childhood memory. They seemed happy.

He began to wander the streets, letting the reality of his situation sink in. Regardless of whether the dream was true or not, he *had* put a knife to the stomach of the woman he loved and his unborn child. That he couldn't deny. He couldn't go back home.

Brennan thought about calling his father to see if he could sleep there, but the memory of his father in the dream made him dismiss that option. Something about it was too real. Now he wished Carson was around, so he could talk to him about everything. Carson was a train wreck, but they were still twins and shared the same experiences. When they were kids, at least. Not after they graduated from high school. Since then, Brennan tried to prove he was put together, while Carson was hell bent on proving he wasn't.

Brennan headed to Carson's place, hoping his brother had left a key hidden under the mat. Carson lived alone in an apartment that at best could be described as a junkie flophouse. It would do for one night.

The apartment was tucked up above a head shop and wasn't much bigger than a closet. Carson was almost never home, anyway, so he made due. Brennan climbed the narrow stairs and stood outside the door. He swore he heard someone moving around inside the apartment and paused before knocking. Was Carson home? Did he lie about going to Ireland?

Brennan tapped lightly, ready to ream his brother if he was in there. Instead, the noise fell quiet, and Brennan doubted he'd ever heard it. No one answered, so he fished around under the doormat. Bingo. The key was there. Carson was shit at keeping track of things, so he often hid things around to find later.

The apartment smelled odd when Brennan pushed open the door. Carson never kept it clean, however, that wasn't it. Musty, but something else, as well. Something earthy and alive.

Brennan stepped in and felt around for the light switch. Something brushed against his hand, and he yanked it back. Sighing, he reached out again, silently admonishing himself for freaking out over a spider web. He found the light and flicked it on, the sight of the apartment causing him to stumble backward into the small landing.

"What the fuck?" he whispered as he gazed into the small space.

The apartment was filled floor to ceiling with some sort of webs. Not spider webs, though. It looked like silk strands stretched from end to end. Brennan stepped forward and touched one. It glistened in the light and felt like fishing line.

What the fuck was Carson up to? Brennan peered closely and could see some sort of pods in the silken maze. No, not pods. Cocoons. Was Carson breeding butterflies?

Brennan stared in amazement as his brain tried to find a logical explanation for what he was seeing. Carson clearly hadn't been home for at least a week, probably more. It dawned on Brennan what was going on. Carson liked to partake in drugs of every kind. Maybe something he bought had eggs in it, and he didn't know. They must have hatched since he was gone.

Thinking about the life cycle of caterpillars, Brennan frowned. Even if there had been eggs for them to hatch, grow into caterpillars, then become cocoons, it couldn't have happened that quickly, could it? Science wasn't Brennan's strong suit, so he couldn't remember anything about the life cycle enough to make a judgment call. Whatever was going on was fucking weird.

"Carson? You in here?" Brennan called out, even though he knew Carson wasn't. He reached out and tugged on one of the strings. It wouldn't break. Carson was going to have a mess on his hands when he got home.

Liquid and bone, never come home.

Brennan shook the words out of his head. He backed out of the door and shut it gently. There was no way he was going to sleep in there now. Even if he could clear the cocoons from the space, it freaked him out. A thought crossed his mind, and he froze.

The doctor said Brennan had some kind of caterpillar or worm in his brain. Did Carson fucking bring something home that then got into Brennan's brain? They didn't see each other much, but they still crossed paths now and again. Did Carson infect him with his tainted drugs? Brennan was going to beat his brother's ass if he did.

Brennan stomped down the stairs, not bothering to check if he'd relocked the door. If anyone tried to break in there, they wouldn't get very far. He stepped onto the sidewalk and glanced around, running out of options.

Tonight had been weird. First the dream, then the knife, now Carson's freaky apartment. Brennan sensed the old urges surfacing and headed to the one place where he felt like he was understood. After a few blocks, he picked up the pace, the pull becoming stronger.

A knock at the door led to it swinging wide after a few seconds. Brennan hoped she was alone. Desiree smiled and tipped her head, glancing past him into the hall, then staring down at his strange attire.

"Had to see me so bad, you didn't even put on your clothes?" she teased.

Brennan realized what a sight he must be standing there and dropped his head. "Sorry, can I come in? I need to talk to someone."

Desiree waved him in. "Not sure how to charge for that, unless you want to roll in the sack first."

Brennan shook his head. "Whatever it costs. You know I don't cheat on my girl."

"Aw, honey, I know you don't, and that's admirable. You want the usual?"

For once, Brennan didn't. He met Desiree's eyes, tears pricking at his. What the hell was happening to him? Desiree reached out and touched his shaved head, brushing the staples still holding his scalp together.

"What happened to you?" she whispered, offering more kindness than he was used to, except from Marly.

"I had something in my brain. They took it out."

Desiree recoiled and took his arm, leading him to a plush velour couch. "Oh, darling, sit down, then. Why are you wandering the streets late at night after brain surgery? Shouldn't you be in the hospital?"

Brennan met her eyes and found a friend. He didn't realize how alone he'd been for so long. Marly would do anything for him, but he felt it was his job to be strong, to take care of her. Desiree sat down next to him and wrapped her arms around him. Brennan let his head rest against her chest and began to sob. She didn't say anything, just kept rubbing his back and humming to him.

Brennan didn't realize he'd fallen asleep until he woke up later, lying on the couch with a soft, purple blanket covering him. He opened his eyes and saw Desiree standing over a small stove, heating up a tea kettle. Something about her was different, and he sat up, rubbing his eyes.

Desiree normally wore a wig and a lot of makeup. Brennan supposed he hadn't registered that before now, since their interactions had always been brief. However, now he saw her for who she truly was.

Desiree turned with a smile. "Awake, sleepyhead?"

Brennan sat up and watched the person who probably knew parts of him best. Yet everything he was seeing was a complete shock to him. Desiree caught him staring and nodded, understanding.

"You didn't notice before now? I am a work in progress."

Work in progress was a good way to explain it. Brennan shook his head. "Sorry, it's none of my business."

"What? That I used to be a man? Honey, that's nothing to worry about. I am on my way to becoming my true self. Nothing to be ashamed of."

Brennan watched her and realized it didn't change anything. Desiree's acceptance of him was something he didn't ever think he would find. "You are beautiful."

Desiree came over and handed him a cup of tea and sat down next to him. "Here. I put a little honey in it. Anyway, I am who I'm meant to be on the bottom and working on who I am up top. However, always been me, always been Desiree. You want a peek?"

Brennan thought about it and nodded. Desiree stood up and stripped. She'd had surgery on the bottom, as she said, but not the top. She spun around, and Brennan ap-

preciated the work in progress as she called it. She slipped back into her clothes and sat down. Brennan found nothing about her that made him uncomfortable. If anything, it made perfect sense. It made him feel at home.

He took her hand and smiled. "Thank you for letting me in, and trusting me with your..."

Secret?

"My metamorphosis, darling."

Metamorphosis. Brennan related to that. He touched his scalp tenderly, thinking about the crazy events of the last week. Something was shifting. Desiree nodded as she stroked his cheek.

"So, my precious child, tell me about what it is you're running from?"

Chapter 12

Flynn comforted me more, his arms wrapped around my frame, bringing me home. I could see his aura, luminous, purple, and radiant. Images from my childhood played like a projector before my eyes, my brother opening Christmas presents by the tree. Our cat Boots wandered past, rubbing against Brennan. My brother looked happy, happier than I ever remember him being.

I saw Dad, and he appeared miserable, focusing on something no one else could see. I wasn't sure what it was, but I could tell he wasn't there with the family. Christmas morning unfolded, and he couldn't care less, something pulling him away from his loved ones. Brennan was ecstatic over whatever the fuck the gift was he'd unwrapped. I couldn't really tell as the flashback fluttered, struggling to make sense of the vision.

We must have been around ten years old, and my Grandma was there, too, watching Dad off in la-la land, before he realized Grandma was eyeing him, a silent message passing between them. It made me uncomfortable, and I couldn't quite put my finger on why.

Grandma's hair covered her face like a black veil, then her eyes began to glow, turning red. I tried to look around for Grandad, but I didn't see him anywhere. Watching Grandma shift into a monster, her teeth growing and becoming foam-infested, made my belly ache.

Everything changed in an instant, my mother appearing again, faintly, a voice in the wind. I missed that sound, something I remembered, like a distant melody.

"You must go home, my sweet child. Liquid and bone will leave you alone," she begged.

I didn't know what that meant as the woods swirled strangely, the stars meeting the horizon. Everything stretched and wobbled, similar to an incessant static, my mother moving to the forefront. The fuzz tried to take her from me, but she spoke again, repeating the phrase like a harrowing mantra. "Carson, my boy, liquid and bone will leave you alone."

"What does that mean? Mother? Please, I'm so lost. I'm broken. Look at me. What is left of me? Who am I anymore? I'm confused without you. Brennan is off starting a new family and thinking less about me, more and more every day. I need you."

"Listen to the music. It's always a sign. You will drown. You will be swallowed up by liquid. It is not the sea you must fear; it is the heat of death you must avoid at all costs. If you stay, you will become a part of the earth. Liquid and bone will leave you alone."

In an instant, she vanished, leaving me all by my lonesome. My mother disappeared into the evening fog like a sprite, gone as if she'd never been there at all.

Flynn sat beside me, holding my hand like the loving father I never had. Comforting me, he acted as an angel guarding me. I could see his wings and feel his beauty in my throat. Tasting his purity on my tongue, I saw the security of a lighthouse in each iris.

"Are you alright, mate?" Flynn asked.

Noticing the love and soul in him, I fell under his spell. His eyes were brown as fallen pinecones, drawing me in. "I'm really high. I think I need to lie down on my back and feel the earth on my skin."

I took my shirt off and felt the cool breeze brush against my chest, making my nipples erect. It felt good, and I caught Flynn gazing at me, taking in my physique. Despite my avid partying and binge drinking, I worked out excessively, often when plastered.

Flynn took note, smiling, his eyes changing from a lighthouse to a burning of an ember.

My thoughts of sex subsided, the LSD opening my thoughts to the delicate lifeforce pumping through me and every living being on this sacred planet. As the forest floor touched my flesh, I recognized the song playing inside, blaring from the crowded home, another favorite of Brennan's. The tune triggered the dream again, and my mother's prophecy.

You are fucking balls deep, Carson. Allow yourself to let go. Take the ground in. Become one with Ireland, allow your Celtic heritage to take root, I thought to myself as the music washed over me.

I tried to focus on the lyrics, the song becoming smells and grotesque imagery. I saw fire, melted flesh, eyes bursting, and my anus defecating. Then, my sense of self shifted. Leaving my body and drifting into the cosmos, my ego fought but surrendered to the drug in charge. I rose high above my body, watching myself in the woods beside the cabin below with Flynn beside me. He held my head in his lap, playing with my hair, reveling in the beauty as I floated further into the aether.

I was weightless, then suddenly I wasn't.

Falling through the void, I could feel layers of myself peeling like an onion.

I unraveled.

Returning to the physical plane felt like a gut punch. I wasn't sure why; my ego no longer wanted a part of this world. I was ready to drift into the heavens to greet my mother and grandfather.

Uncontrolled, I returned.

"You back?" Flynn whispered.

"Yeah, I think so. This shit has me so fucked up. I need a drink, I think. Something to take the edge off."

"Do you want beer or liquor?" Flynn asked, the full moon catching the angles of his face as he smiled.

I caught my breath, wanting more of the lines around his mouth. Angelic and truly divine, Flynn captivated me in ways I'd never experienced. For the first time in my life, I wondered if I was in love.

CHAPTER 13

IN DESIREE, BRENNAN FOUND something he'd never been able to wrap his mind around. It wasn't sexual, even if she teased him about it often. It was more than that. It was home. Brennan felt deep shame for bailing on Marly like he did, but he was afraid that if he stayed, he would unintentionally harm her. Desiree let him crash on her couch for a few days to get his bearings. She often had clients throughout the day, and he'd take a walk while they were there. She'd open the curtains when the client left to let him know it was safe to come back.

He'd been honest with her about everything that first night. Things he'd pushed to the darkest recesses of his mind.

About his mother, the dream he had about his father and grandmother killing her. The distance that had grown between him and Carson. How he dreaded the birth of his own daughter and felt like her first breath might be his last. About waking up with a knife to Marly's belly, even though she meant more to him than anything else in the world. Desiree didn't laugh or tell him that what he was feeling wasn't valid.

She just listened.

However, on the third day, Desiree woke him up, sitting on the edge of the couch. Brennan saw her and blinked a few times to let his eyes adjust to the light and allow his brain to take in his surroundings. Desiree was in her house garb, no makeup, no wig. She gave him a sad smile.

"You need to go get your life back in order," she said kindly, making it clear it wasn't an option not to.

Brennan sat up and nodded. "I know. You're right. This isn't fair to Marly."

"Have you spoken with her?"

Brennan ran his hand through his hair and shrugged. "I called her. She was pissed to say the least."

Desiree glanced away, staring out the window. "Wouldn't you be? If the person you loved and were having a child with took off when you needed them most. When they were injured and vulnerable? She must be worried. Sometimes worry comes out as anger."

Brennan knew she was right. He needed to face Marly. He couldn't stay at the apartment until he knew what was going on with him, though. He loved Marly, even if it meant losing her. He shifted on the couch and touched

Desiree's hand. "Thank you, Des. For letting me stay, for talking to me. I'm all kinds of fucked up, right now."

"That won't change, honey, not until you face what is tormenting you. You need to go back, if nothing more than to be honest with that woman of yours. I'll make you breakfast, but then you need to leave."

It sounded harsher than she meant, and she smiled and brushed his cheek with her fingers as she stood up. Brennan understood. Latching onto the next person who would listen wouldn't solve his problems. He needed to deal with them and treat Marly the way she deserved.

After breakfast, Brennan hopped in the shower and threw on the clothes he'd come in wearing, pajamas really. Desiree had tossed them in the wash, and he appreciated her for that. He didn't want to go home smelling like body odor or whatever perfume Desiree doused her apartment in.

The walk home was long, and he found himself dragging his feet the closer he got. He fully expected Marly to rip him a new one when he got there. However, once he got to the apartment, he was surprised to find it empty. A note was on the counter that made him want to bawl.

Bren,

I don't know what's going on with you, but it isn't healthy for me to stay here while you ignore our baby and me. I have gone to stay with my mother for a while. I think it's best. I love you with every fiber of my being, but I won't allow you to treat me like I don't exist. I have given you everything, and you find it so easy to disregard me. I don't know if you are confiding in someone else, but I don't deserve this. You need to grow up and stop running to everyone else. You pushed Carson away; now you are pushing me away. The more you love someone, the more you cast them off. It hurts, and it isn't fair. I need someone who honors me and wants a partner.

I hope you find what you are looking for. I hope our child means enough to you to be there for her. I can't promise I will still want you, though. I need someone who nurtures and respects me. Respects our bond. Right now, that isn't you.

Marly

Not signed love, only her name as a final reminder of everything he was throwing away. He wouldn't chase after her or call her mother's house. He knew she was completely right in her assessment, and now he was even more ashamed. He turned to Desiree instead of being honest with the one person who mattered to him more than anything in the world. Even so, he couldn't ignore the fact that he had put a knife to her belly. To their daughter.

He packed a bag and wrote a note in response, then considered throwing it away. She might not even come back to the apartment. He tapped his fingers on the counter, then signed his name.

Marly,

I'm so sorry, you didn't deserve any of this. I love you, please know that. More than I could ever explain. I know it's not enough right now. There's something I need to do to be the man you should have in your life. To be the father our daughter deserves. I can't tell you what's going on, but please believe me when I say it's for the best if I leave for a while. You are better off with your mother. I'm sorry.

Love,
Brennan

He'd taken that risk. He stopped by the mailbox on his way out and reached in, his hands brushing something foreign. He jerked his hand out and peered in. There was a postcard in the box, but it was covered with webs, like the ones in Carson's place. He frowned and eased the postcard out, seeing it was from his brother.

A simple message, yet it weighed heavily on him. He *had* pushed Carson away. It was easier to see his brother as a fuck up than to admit he was just as damaged and lost.

He ran his fingers over the scrawled writing and felt a pang of loneliness. He missed Carson.

As he shut the mailbox door, he knew he needed to make another stop, as much as he dreaded it. He headed uptown on the bus and got off at the one place he didn't want to be. He walked a few blocks and came to the sliding glass doors. They opened too easily as if to say, "Come in and take your punishment."

The rush of artificial air hit his face as he entered, and he fought back a sneeze. The girl at the front desk barely looked up as he signed in, showed his ID, and made his way down the disinfected halls. His grandmother's door was cracked open, and Brennan took a deep breath.

He really didn't want to be here.

She was sleeping with her head turned toward the window. Even in rest, his grandmother appeared unhappy. Her dark brows were a stark contrast against her pale, thin skin. Brennan eased over to the end of the bed and cleared his throat as he stared at her.

"Grandma, are you awake?"

She flinched but didn't open her eyes. She was awake, but ignoring him. Brennan felt anger rise in him and shook her bed in disgust. She had always been that way. Unreachable. He wouldn't allow it this time.

"Wake up, Grandma, I'm not leaving until you do."

She shifted and let her eyes open a slit. What sounded like a guttural grunt escaped her body, and she turned her head toward him, a strange smile forming on her lips.

"What do you want, boy?"

Brennan felt the temperature in the room shift and swore she never blinked. He almost lost his nerve, then thought about Marly and Carson. He moved to the side of her bed. "I need you to tell me what happened to my mother. To my sister."

The old woman glanced at the door as if she expected a visitor, then narrowed her eyes at him. "Don't ask questions for answers you don't want, Edgar."

Edgar was his grandfather's name, so this threw Brennan off. While his grandmother often forgot this, she seemed lucid and was calling him by his grandfather's name. Rather than correct her, Brennan leaned closer. "Tell me, you old, miserable bitch."

If she was shocked by his comment, she didn't show it. Instead, she laughed and grabbed his hand, squeezing it harder than a woman her age should be able to. In that moment, her face changed, and he saw the being that hovered over him night after night, taunting him. As quickly as it came, it shifted back to her face, and her eyes locked on his with a mixture of disdain and rage.

"She wasn't family. She was a temptress who lured your father away. I tolerated you boys because you were sons.

Boys carry the family blood, however, I was not going to allow a filthy girl to mess everything up."

A filthy girl? His sister? His grandmother was out of her mind, but even this was out of left field. "You killed my mother because she was having a girl baby?"

The old woman cackled and dug her nails into Brennan's hand, breaking the skin. "It had to be done. Your father understood. Girls break the bloodline. Girls must be killed if their blood is tainted."

Tainted blood. What the hell was she talking about? Brennan yanked his hand free and glared at his grandmother. She'd just admitted to him, she and his father had killed his mother and sister. Brennan felt the room begin to spin and could swear he felt something crawling around in his brain. He reached out to brace himself on the bed rail as he fell to his knees.

The old woman continued laughing, then whispered, "Good thing Carson left, the land will take care of him. He is tainted, as well, and it'll be better for what happens to him. Cleanse the family blood."

Brennan began to understand what she was saying. Carson wouldn't survive his trip to Ireland. He stumbled to his feet and lurched out the door, hearing the evil woman he thought was family whisper over and over.

"Liquid and bone, never come home."

He made it to the street before he vomited, startling a woman coming up to the building. He put his hand up to let her know he was alright and staggered toward the bus stop. If he'd had any doubts about what to do, he didn't now. In order to save everyone who mattered to him, he needed to do something he'd been fighting against all along.

By eleven o'clock that night, Brennan O'Leary was on a flight to Ireland. To figure out his family history and secrets, so he could put them behind him. It was the only way he could protect Marly and his daughter. He needed to stop running from the truth he thought would stay buried as long as he pretended it didn't exist.

First, though, he needed to accept the part of him he'd been ignoring. The other half of him he'd tried to sever, creating his own suffering as a result.

He needed to find Carson.

Chapter 14

Flynn looked at me with those pinecone eyes of his, and the whole world melted away. Every bit of the cosmos twinkled in his presence. Enamored, awestruck, and ready to fully commit to a life with him, never in my wildest dreams did I ever think I'd feel this way about someone. I wanted to be a different person, to change the most difficult parts of myself, all while having the desire to be the person everyone in my past told me I could be.

With Flynn, I didn't sulk, moving like a battered critter, even if right now I acted like one. Drugs do that, though. I can't explain it. Around him, I buckle, ready to follow him to the sea, a river, a mountain, anywhere, even if it means death.

Intoxicating, pale, and perfect like the moon, his skin sucked my soul into a whirlwind. The trail of freckles down his arms reminded me of constellations, making me wonder who painted them on him. He was a work of art. I never wanted anything more in my life. His belly button swirled like a maelstrom, beckoning me to descend below it. The urge felt different. I wasn't used to it.

Usually, when I felt a connection with another person, it was purely sexual, but this powerful force was a different kind of beast. Full of primal energy and animalistic hunger, it commanded every bit of my anatomy. It pulsed and throbbed, and I felt it in my groin, limbs, heart, and head. I want to dive headfirst into lust and extreme intimacy, my desire for Flynn overwhelming me, bringing me to my knees. More than desire, I was caught in his energy, being dragged willingly into him.

"I'm going to get you a drink. Stay here, sit, and just breathe. It will all be okay," Flynn assured me, walking back into the house.

I wanted him more as he disappeared inside. Seeing Flynn leave broke me. Sitting there alone, I looked at my hands and feet. They were oversized, then infantile. I saw myself as a baby and a man all at once. Trying to make sense of this strange reality, I struggled, unsure what was happening to me, but it felt cosmic. My brain churned desperately, my thoughts raced like the wind, and I questioned my entire existence.

What if all of this were to lead me here? To Flynn? What if it's all connected? What if the universe had this in motion from the moment I was born, no, conceived?

What if it's all one incredible orchestra? Grandad dying, then me coming here to Ireland, going to the club, meeting whatever his fucking name is at the bar, then meeting Flynn. What if this is it? This is why I'm here. Flynn.

Flynn's the one.

The thought consumed me. It made too much sense, yet none at all. I couldn't tell today from a decade ago. My life began to mold into something so much more than me. I saw myself in the stars, moon, constellations, and trees. The ley lines of Earth penetrating my feet the moment I removed my shoes. Blades of grass graced my soles, and I wiggled my toes, squashing organic debris freely between them.

"Earth loves you, and you are being guided by love," I whispered to the sky, the words evaporating off my lips as soon as they were released. As I spoke, a breeze rustled through the trees, as if to say, "I'm listening."

Mother Nature plucked the strings, and I resonated, creating glorious harmonies all over the Irish countryside. I saw my heart create patterns, images of the solar system emerging from eyelids. "This is it. This is why you are here. This is why you exist."

As the words left my mouth, Flynn returned with a pint in hand and a glass of water. He sat down next to me. "Here. Drink this first, then you can have the beer. You need to stay hydrated, mate," he insisted.

Taking the water from his hand and placing it on the ground, I kissed him. Deep and passionate. I exerted the most emotion I'd ever put into anything in my life. I felt eons of time rush through my body, through my cells. I experienced the waves of the ocean crashing against cliffs and volcanoes spewing molten lava from deep within the caverns of planet Earth.

"Fuck, no one's ever kissed me quite like that before," Flynn uttered, pulling his lips from mine, his eyes deep with emotion. "Damn, where'd you learn to kiss like that?"

He laughed, and I smiled slightly back at him, hoping not to reveal my inner turmoil. I could feel myself giving in to the forces at work. I didn't want to.

"Too much practice," I said.

"Well, practice makes perfect. You can kiss me like that anytime," he whispered.

"Yeah, is that right?"

"Yeah."

Crickets chirped, and the rhythm of their song sounded sporadic but gentle, soothing the angst inside me. I could hear the buzzing and the space between the vibrations. There in the emptiness, a light, the beacon through the darkness, called out. I listened, tuning into the natural ambiance bustling on the ground and in the air. The more the insects stirred around me, the more focused I became.

I noticed a moth moving toward the lights flickering by the back porch. Colorful bits of white, citron, and green sparkled in its wide wings.

"What are you looking at?" Flynn asked.

I pointed to the moth in the light, my mouth no longer part of my body—the acid and the alcohol making me less human. Words were difficult to string together as every minute ticked by.

"That's a killer-looking moth," Flynn mentioned, moving closer to examine it. "I'm a bit nocturnal myself," he added, almost to himself.

As he leaned into the insect, I could see his aura, splashes of purple and indigo, moving like a wave in the sea. Flynn was everything, and I was nothing, the moth trapped by his eternal flame. Calling me, calling me. I got up and joined him.

"I don't care about some moth, with you standing there," I said, wrapping my arms around his muscular body and slipping my tongue into his mouth.

We made out for a while before Flynn offered to head to his place further out in the country. An offer that got my blood pumping.

"It's twenty minutes further into the Wicklow mountains. It's small, but it's enough for you and me," Flynn suggested.

"Whatever gets me closer to you," I replied, gazing into the swirling mass of brown beaming from his eyes.

I knew I was high. I knew this with my core. However, that far out and that far deep in a trip, the universe lured me in, and I was spread across the entire cosmos. My ego only wanted Flynn, but there seemed to be something in my heart battling against this drive, this pull between Flynn and me.

"Let's go," he murmured in a sincere and direct voice, like a stern but loving father.

He reminded me of my Dad. They both were aloof but direct, and that was the feeling I got from Flynn. I hated it, but in a lot of ways, he also reminded me of my mother. He had the gentle, nurturing side she offered during her short time with Brennan and me.

We walked away from the home. As we were descending the hill, the sounds of binge drinking echoed behind us, and I heard the music increase in volume. At first, I thought someone inside had turned up the stereo, but I quickly realized it was me controlling the sound. The LSD worked its magic and made me feel like a sorcerer. I honed in on the tune playing between my ears and recognized it as Shadowplay by Joy Division. Another band my twin and I loved dearly.

My twin...

For a moment, my soul ached. I thought of Brennan and the days of being in the city, back in the States, partying and hanging out. Back then, we lived a few blocks from each other. He wasn't dating Marly then, rather a girl named Clara. She was the opposite of Marly, more like me, impulsive and spontaneous. A heavy drinker and kind of lush, Brennan and Clara didn't last long, but she was a big Joy Division fan.

When Ian Curtis killed himself, we were all distraught. The band was about to embark on their first North American tour from England, and we were fired up, then crushed by the terrible news.

We gathered at Brennan's apartment to drink and do drugs. Clara and I did loads of cocaine and smoked joint after joint while Brennan watched us from the sofa, not being a fan of the hard stuff.

At one point, things got out of hand, and I kissed Clara. Brennan flipped out, and we got into a physical altercation. He threw me into the wall and busted my nose pretty good, after he snuck in a free, cheap shot. I apologized for months, telling him I'd been really fucked up. He broke it off with Clara the next day, and it took a couple of years for the wound between us to mend. It wasn't until he met Marly that we grew close again, if that's what it could be called.

The song made me feel sad, a hefty sorrow, and I did what I did best: chugged the rest of my booze and reached into my pocket for the remaining coke. Anything to bury the pain, to escape the feeling.

"Hold on. Let's finish off this powder before we lose the light from the party," I suggested, handing Flynn my miniature compact mirror. We stood under the moonlight between worlds.

I sprinkled some onto the glass and let him do the honors. That was new for me; I always ripped my drugs first, especially when I paid for them. Again, Flynn was different, so different. He did his bump and held the mirror while I rocketed mine. We both rubbed our noses, letting the cocaine drip down our throats.

"Are you good now?" Flynn asked.

I smiled and didn't say anything back. I kissed him, then looked across the landscape. The shadows were mingling around us with intensity.

I climbed into his car, and we started the trip further into the hills. Flynn hit the gas, and off we went. The buzz felt fantastic as we drove. I could see a spool of energy spilling out of my chest as we headed down the road. The stars shone like diamonds in the sky. I tried to pull them from the quilt of obsidian drenched above, but they were much too far away.

I lit a smoke and handed it to Flynn, then lit another for myself. He turned up the music as we cruised. I began to feel anxious the closer we got to his house. Figuring it was the coke, I tried to relax, but once we pulled in the driveway, it felt like a full-blown panic attack. I hyperventilated and gasped for air, seeing stars all around me.

"Just breathe," Flynn whispered, as he held my hand. We sat in the car as he comforted me. "Just breathe."

Chapter 15

Brennan dozed on the plane after catching his connecting flight out of New York. His mind raced, and panic was doing its best to burrow deep down into his chest. After the last interaction with his grandmother, Brennan knew Carson was in trouble. Hell, they both were. If she and his father were willing to kill Brennan's mother and baby sister, there was no telling what else they were willing to do. His whole life had been a lie, and the people he trusted were not who he believed they were.

They were dangerous... evil.

He knew he should have gone to the police before boarding the plane to tell them about what happened to his mother and sister, however, something told him he needed to get his feet on Irish soil before he lost the only sibling he had left. He needed to find his brother. He clutched Carson's postcard in his hand as he slept, hoping it would somehow connect him to his missing twin.

Turbulence jostled Brennan awake, and he peered around the dimly lit cabin. Most of the other passengers were sleeping or reading, and all he could hear was the soft chatter of the flight attendants a few rows up. They were sitting with their heads leaned together, whispering so as not to disturb the passengers. Brennan's ears turned into their words, and the hair stood up on his arms as he heard what they were saying to one another.

"At least this flight is quiet, not like my last one to Ireland. Remember that crazy guy on that flight?" one of them said quietly.

"The one with the dark hair who was freaking out? Was he on something?" the blond replied.

"He had to be. He was cute, but he was off his rocker. I wonder what happened to him once he got off the plane."

"Ireland swallowed him whole," the blond flight attendant answered, then chuckled. "These Americans always think they are going home when they go to Ireland. Like it's some special fucking calling."

Brennan knew they were talking about Carson. He strained to hear more, but they moved on to some other gossip, and he stared out the window. It was night, and they were over the ocean. There wasn't much to view, but he could see the moonlight glistening off the vast sea. A wave of anxiety passed over him, and he closed his eyes.

At least he was on the right path. If Carson had taken a previous flight, Brennan was following his brother's trail.

He fell back into a restless sleep and dreamed of a time when they were children. Their mother had taken them to the beach and was laughing as they made unsuccessful attempts to build a sandcastle. She was pregnant at the time, but got down in the sand with them and showed her boys how to create a moat first to catch the water, so they could build the sandcastle without the waves destroying their hard work.

"See, like this?" she said as she scooped handfuls of sand out in a large ring. She placed the sand in the center of the mounds. "Now use these piles to make the sandcastle."

The boys hopped the moat and set about making their structure. Their mother closed her eyes as she lay back on her chair with her hand resting on her belly. That was the memory, but the dream carried it on, creating a new, darker ending.

Carson ran toward the water, laughing with his head back. Brennan didn't want to go swimming; he wanted to keep building the sandcastle. Yet, in the next scene, he was knee-deep in the water, and their mother was gone from the beach. So was Carson. Brennan peered around and saw a flash of skin under the turbulent waves.

Carson!

Brennan realized his twin was drowning and dove into the water to save him. The ocean was full of thick seaweed, and Brennan kept getting tangled in it, being dragged down below the surface. He waved his arms around him under the water, trying to find his brother.

His hands landed on something solid, and he drew it toward him. It didn't feel like skin, but it was heavy. Brennan struggled with the weight and aggressive seaweed as he dragged the shape to the shore. He felt his feet hit sand and began to lurch toward dry land. Once he got there, he dropped the large, cold item and stared at it. It seemed to be a sheath of thick seaweed, wrapped around something. Something moving! Whatever was inside was alive and trying to get out.

Brennan began to peel back layers of the seaweed and saw skin. He recognized the mole on the upper arm and realized Carson was trapped in the vegetation and suffocating. Brennan began to desperately rip the layers off his brother, hoping he could free him in time.

By the time he got Carson free, his twin was no longer breathing, and Brennan threw himself down on his knees, pounding on Carson's chest. His brother's eyes stared vacantly at the darkening sky. Brennan was too late.

Carson was dead.

Brennan jerked awake in his seat and gasped loudly. Nearby passengers stared at him in shock, and the two flight attendants he'd heard talking earlier glanced at him, then at each other as if to decide if they had another problem passenger on their hands. Since Brennan and Carson looked so different, they didn't put the connection together, however, they were leery of yet another freak-out.

Brennan put his hand in the air. "Sorry, just a bad dream. I get anxious when flying."

The blond one eyed him, then nodded with a practiced smile. "We are almost there, sir. Another few minutes and we will be getting ready for our descent."

Brennan nodded at her, then looked at the postcard in his hand. Was he too late? He conjured Carson in his mind, but nothing came back, either way. It was like Carson had simply vanished from the world. Thoughts of Marly crossed his mind, and incredible guilt washed over him. A thin, wispy thought crossed his mind, and the hair on his neck began to prickle. He couldn't quite catch it, but he knew it was a warning. About what, he didn't know.

The plane's wheels hit the tarmac, and Brennan felt a strange sensation. A pull. As if the cells were being drawn through his pores. He shook his head and pushed the feeling away. Once the plane came to a stop at the gate and the other passengers began to gather their belongings, Brennan had an image of Marly again. She was rubbing her belly and whispering to the child inside. His mother's face replaced Marly's, and she stared up, her eyes black and hollow. Brennan rose out of his seat too quickly and smacked his head on the low ceiling below the baggage hold.

"Ow, fuck," he whispered as a woman with her child scurried by, giving him a dirty look.

Was Marly in danger? Brennan was conflicted. His brother was missing, and now he was worried about Marly's safety, as well. She was at her mother's, which was good. No one in his family knew where her mother lived. He didn't want to scare her, but he also needed her to know not to interact with his family. He'd call her from the airport.

As he stepped off the plane through the gate, alarms were going off in his head. Telling him to turn around and go back to the United States. Brennan paused, and a man walking behind him, who was looking at his ticket, ran into the back of him.

"What the hell, dude," the man muttered and moved around him, not looking back.

Brennan pushed the anxiety down and continued into the airport. He couldn't turn around because he didn't have a flight for a week. He needed to find Carson and bring him home. First, though, he needed to call Marly.

As suspected, she didn't answer, so he left a message, hoping she would get it as soon as possible. "Hey, Marly, it's Brennan. I'm in Ireland. I'm going to find Carson and bring him home. Listen, I had a falling out with my family. Please don't contact them or interact with them. I found out something they did, and I don't trust them. Stay at your mother's until I get home. I love you, Mar. Please know that. More than anything in the world. I'm sorry I've been such an asshole. I have been struggling with some stuff mentally lately. I promise when I get home, I'll be the man and the father you and the baby deserve. I love you."

He hung up and gazed around the airport, not sure what to do next. Carson had been there; he could feel it. Where did he go once he left? Brennan went to pick up his bags and wandered out of the airport once he had his belongings. It was nighttime. He peered around the area, trying to think like his brother.

A taxi driver standing nearby waved at him with a look of disinterest. "You need a ride, boy?"

Brennan nodded, knowing his next stop. "Yeah, I do. Thank you. Can you take me to the nearest pub?"

Think like Carson.

Chapter 16

The drugs kept me in a headlock. I couldn't tell where reality ended and fantasy began. All I knew was that Flynn sat with me the whole time, keeping his palm on my back, providing gentle pats of security. I found insurmountable solace in him. In all my years of lusting, no one came close. This was the man I wanted. I didn't want a woman, or any other man, only Flynn and Flynn alone. His grasp on my soul felt ancient, blossoming from a place of sincerity. Staring at him as my anxiety passed, I saw my knight in shining armor, my comfort blanket, a lantern.

I bowed to his every flicker.

We sat there on the steps of the small abode in silence, only the sound of the trees rustling in the breeze. I heard my mother along the wind, speaking softly. *Liquid and bone will leave you alone.*

Peering at Flynn, in that moment, he changed. His eyes grew red, and his skin turned grey. He looked old and evil, the energy coming off him dark and unsettling. I knew the drugs were fucking with me. Shaking off the terrible visuals, I hugged him and pushed my fears into the abyss, running my fingers through Flynn's hair.

"You better, mate? Wanna go in? It's getting cold out here. Let's have a pint and warm up," he offered.

"Yeah, thanks for understanding. I have so much going on, and it all hit me all at once. I think I'm suppressing my grief, missing my brother, and wondering where things went wrong, even though I know I had a lot to do with it. Then there's my mother, who died when we were really young. I barely remember her most times. She's like a dream. You know, you remind me a little of her," I said, crossing the threshold of the home.

Flynn's house was dark, but inviting as he fumbled with a lamp switch before flicking it on to reveal the clean and simple decor. The walls were bare, and the floors were well swept. The place smelled like mothballs, causing me to wonder if his grandparents lived there. Oddly basic, but warm with a comfy couch, a small kitchen, and a tiny bedroom in the back next to a cramped bathroom.

"Grab a seat, I'll get you a pint," Flynn suggested, opening the fridge.

He stumbled back in, then handed me a Guinness. Taking it, my bracelet glistened in the lamplight—the, *C* attached to it jingling like a bell. I couldn't shake how mundane the home seemed. It felt more like an afterthought than a place to unwind and relax. It lacked depth, with no character to it, which I found strange because Flynn had so much personality. I assumed his place would reflect that.

"Where are all the posters of naked guys on the walls?" I joked.

Flynn didn't seem to pay my comment any mind and continued sipping his stout. My anxiety crept in. I'd overdone it with the drugs and no sleep, and now, I was paying the price.

"Show me your bedroom," I mentioned, surveying the home for an indication that it had been lived in. There were no personal possessions. I didn't see clothes or album collections. No record player or tape deck, no television or radio. Nothing that made it a home.

"Sure, it isn't much," Flynn said, leading the way to the back room.

"This place isn't shit. Where's your stuff?"

"I'm not much for possessions," Flynn added, opening the bedroom door. The space smelled bizarre, a strange mixture of sweat, piss, and mold. I gagged when it hit my nose, my eyes watering in rebellion.

"What's that smell?" I asked, covering my nose, trying not to puke.

"Oh, I had a bad mold problem and had to treat it. The smells still linger. That's why I'm not using the backroom right now," he said while flipping on a lamp. Traces of light allowed me to see what created the terrible smell. Along the ceiling and in the corners of the room sat intricate webs. They were spindly, resembling silk, with stringy and fibrous material, the lamplight causing the webbing to shimmer—iridescent yet peculiar.

"What the fuck?" I whispered.

"See, mold?" Flynn huffed.

My head spun. I felt weak and lightheaded. I reached for Flynn's hand, my palms sweaty, and my heart racing. Something wasn't right.

"I need to sit down," I told him.

"Whatever you need to do, my friend. I still can't believe you're here with me finally."

Flynn's words were startling, sending waves of confusion through my core. Growing weaker, my knees buckled as I tried to leave the bedroom. The space became hot and humid, and I could see condensation dripping down the walls, triggering thoughts of my mother.

Liquid and bone will leave you alone.

The room morphed, the space becoming claustrophobic. I could feel the walls closing in on me. The webbing spread, moving along the ceiling like a snake. I saw the spindly threads reaching for me like vines.

I was losing my mind.

The drugs consumed me, and reality dwindled. I knew if I stayed in the house, I'd collapse. I mustered up the energy to run out of the room and out of the house, but Flynn followed me. I leaned over, coughing.

"Are you alright?" he asked.

"No, I'm not. I'm losing it. Something is going on with me. I'm breaking down or some shit."

"Hey, sit down and breathe. Remember? Breathe, Carson, you have a lot going on, and you have a head full of acid and a nose caked with cocaine, mate. What did you expect would happen?"

"You're right."

"Sip your pint, and let the alcohol curb your anxiety," Flynn suggested. "Settle a little."

"I need to move around. I'm feeling antsy. I don't know what I saw in your room, but I didn't like it. It was twisted and felt like a womb in there."

"You remember being in the womb? That's wild. Let's take a walk to clear your head. We can follow the moonlight along the path. There's a cool bog a half a mile away, wanna check it out? It's pretty and has an ancient Celtic feel to it. Americans love going there," Flynn told me.

"Yeah, okay. That sounds nice. I would go anywhere with you," I replied, pulling Flynn in, who led the way with me following closely behind, holding his hand.

Moving through the thicket with ease, Flynn seemed to know the path with the least resistance. We turned a bend, down a corridor of trees to a lush knoll perched beside a bog, the twilight glittering off the water. Limbs reached out of the placid surface, clawing at the air above.

"It's beautiful, isn't it?" Flynn murmured, but something in his voice was different.

"It is," I replied, admiring the calm, opaque water laid out before me.

Something seemed off. I couldn't put my finger on it, but Flynn's energy changed. A shiver passed through me. I could feel his arm around me and his palm on my right shoulder. When I looked up at him, the sight of his face startled me. No longer Flynn, he'd changed into an old woman, reminiscent of my grandmother. Naked and elderly, the folds of wrinkly skin flapped off her feeble arms. Bony and shriveled, her black eyes pulsed like the blue veins running through her translucent skin.

I tried to scream, but my body became paralyzed. I could feel something crawling up my arm. It was the webbing from Flynn's bedroom, stretching out of the bog and wrapping around my ankles. The rug of reality pulled out from beneath me as my body hit the earth.

Being dragged across the forest floor and into the bog, I disappeared under the water, catching a glimpse of the old woman turning into a creature. She shrank and twisted into a tiny winged being with a peculiar green glow. Like that, I vanished, sinking below the surface.

CHAPTER 17

THE PUB WAS AN absolute shithole, weirdly flanked by a McDonald's. Brennan wasn't sure why he was surprised. He'd told the cab driver to take him to a nearby pub, and this place was that, but not much else. He let his eyes adjust to the dim lighting of the pub after paying the driver and sidled up to the bar. Regardless, a cold beer would go down nice right about now. He kept his head low and ordered a beer, not wanting to get into a conversation about being American. The bartender seemed happy to oblige and slide a thick, dark stout across the sticky wooden surface toward Brennan.

The drink was delicious, however, definitely not cold. Not by American standards, but he sipped on it, anyway, glancing around. The hole-in-the-wall pub was definitely for locals as it didn't scream Irish in a cheesy way. It could be a bar on any side street in the United States. Except everything about it seemed old. Like it had been there for hundreds of years.

Brennan took his beer and made his way to a small table in the back corner. His bag was heavy, and standing at the bar with it made him stick out like a sore thumb. After a few more sips of the stout, he began to relax and consider his next steps. If Carson had been there, where would he have gone next?

Knowing Carson, he would have tried to score. Drugs, sex, whatever. Drugs didn't seem to be flowing in the tiny pub, so Brennan peered around at the clientele. Mostly older Irish men, looking like they were avoiding going home for the night. A few ladies, but they weren't dolled up for a good time.

Well, except the redhead at the end of the bar.

She swayed slightly on the stool like she was moving to music no one else could hear. She dangled one leg off the stool as if she were ready to get up and dance.

She was stacked. Curvy and dressed to play up those curves. Her pale breasts looked like at any moment they could spill out of the neck of her black dress, and her hips made the fabric appear like it was an extension of her. She knew it, too, as she rubbed the cocktail straw across her lush lips and gazed around.

His eyes landed on Brennan and stayed too long. He stared down at his beer, not trying to send her the wrong message. She was beautiful but not his type. Marly was fit but never forced her body into a mold. She could be wearing sweatpants and a t-shirt and look sexier to him than any woman dressed to the nines. Even so, he needed information, and if Carson had been there when that woman was, he would've made a beeline for her.

When Brennan glanced up, she was gone, her stool still rocking from her movement. He peered around the bar, but it appeared she'd left.

"Damnit," he grumbled as he finished his beer and got ready to leave. He was exhausted and needed to find a place to bed down for the night. He gathered his bag, paid his tab, and asked the bartender about nearby hotels.

The bartender shook his head. "Not much around here, yeah? Back by the airport are some hotels. There is a bed and breakfast a block over, if that's what you want. Fi will take good care of you and is a hell of a cook."

Brennan considered that and really didn't want to go back to the airport. He asked the bartender to write down directions to the B&B and tipped generously. With the paper in hand, he stepped out into the night and yawned. He felt like it had been night for days. He glanced at the paper and began heading in the direction of the bed and breakfast when he heard an odd noise to his right.

Startled, he jerked his eyes in the direction of the sound, and a shadow stepped out of the darkness into the light. It was the redheaded woman from the bar. She'd gone out first, and him right after, so he didn't want her thinking he was following her.

"Sorry," he muttered, making himself seem less of a threat, and tried to give her a wide berth.

Instead, she moved closer.

"I'm Brianna. Are you American?"

Considering she might be a prostitute, Brennan decided to make it clear he wasn't looking for a good time. "I am. Looking for my brother. I have a girlfriend and a baby on the way."

Brianna laughed dismissively. "Alright, then? Is your brother lost?"

Brennan shook his head, then paused as he thought about the question. Was Carson lost? "I don't know. He came here to find our roots, I think."

"You think? Don't you know why your brother came halfway around the world? Are you two not close?"

Her questions seemed intrusive, and this made Brennan uncomfortable. Who was this lady? "My twin. We're fine. I couldn't come at first because of the baby. Have you seen any Americans come through here recently?"

Brianna tipped her head, her eyes hiding something. "I have. What's your brother's name?"

"Carson. Carson O'Leary."

If Brianna recognized the name, she did a good job of not showing it. She twirled a strand of red hair between her fingers and eyed him suspiciously. "Hmmm. Twins, you say? The only Carson I met looks nothing like you, so I don't think so."

Her demeanor had shifted, and she was no longer acting seductive. Now she was watching Brennan with a mixture of distrust and annoyance.

"Yeah, we don't look alike. Fraternal, not identical. Carson looks like our dad, and I look like our mom. Oh, hold on. I have a picture of him."

Brennan reached into his pocket for his wallet and drew out a tattered photo. It was from their high school graduation. Carson was gazing off like he was fucked up, his cap and gown askew. Brennan, on the other hand, was meeting the camera dead on, his shoulders back and a grin that said he was on the precipice of something great.

He wasn't.

Brianna took the photo and peered closer. Brennan swore he saw a look of recognition in her eyes, but she smiled and shook her head. "Not sure. Have you considered maybe he doesn't want to be found?"

Something about her made Brennan's hackles rise, and he took a step back. She might be beautiful on the outside, however, there was something very ugly about her. Poisonous. He suspected she knew more than she was letting on, but he had no way to prove it. He slipped the picture back into his wallet and smiled.

"Well, it was nice to meet you. Was it Brianna? I need to head on to my accommodations and get some rest. If you happen to see my brother around, can you let him know I am staying at Fiona's Bed and Breakfast for the night?"

She didn't reply and turned and walked away, swinging her hips as if to say he was missing out. Brennan sighed and shifted his bag on his shoulder. When he glanced back at Brianna's retreating form, something stopped him from moving. It was as if her body had morphed. No longer sexy. Her back was hunched, and her arms dangled too far down her body. Her legs, once shapely and smooth, seemed twisted and bony.

Brennan resisted the urge to run away and stared at her for a moment, trying to understand what he was seeing. The blare of a car horn snapped him out of the trance, and he glanced in the direction of the sound. When he looked back, Brianna was gone.

Exhaustion. He was seeing shit because he was tired from traveling and everything leading up to it. He needed to get into a room and close his eyes for a bit. Maybe call Marly. What time was it back home? Rhode Island seemed more than a world away. He stumbled down the road toward the bed and breakfast, hoping someone would be awake to let him check in.

The bartender must have given Fiona a heads-up as she was sitting on the front porch, rocking, when he came down the path. He'd pictured an old woman, but this woman was no older than forty and stunning in a simple way. She was dressed in a knee-length, black skirt with a white blouse, smoking what appeared to be a cigar. She stubbed it out and rose from her seat when Brennan came up the stairs.

"There you are," she said as if she'd been expecting him all along. She gestured to the door. "Come on, then. You must be tired."

He followed her into a small foyer, and she clicked on a lamp. "Mikey told me you were on your way and that you looked beat to hell. I put some fresh towels in the room if you'd like to take a shower."

It was all too familiar, and Brennan began to wonder if he was still on the plane and dreaming. He smiled and set his bag down. "Thank you. I can't tell you how much it means that you were still awake."

"I wasn't, but never mind that. Couldn't leave you out wandering the streets, could I? The room is up the stairs, second door on the right, bathroom across the hall. We can settle up in the morning. I serve breakfast starting at seven. No rush, it is available until checkout, which is eleven."

Brennan stood awkwardly, then glanced up the stairs. "Second door on the right?"

"That's the one. My room is down here, past the kitchen. If you need anything, just knock. I'm a light sleeper."

"Thank you again, I was worried I'd have to sleep on the sidewalk," he replied and chuckled to himself.

Either she didn't understand he was joking or didn't care. She tipped her head. "Have a good night."

Brennan started up the stairs, then paused and turned back. "Do you know a woman around here named Brianna? Goes to the pub?"

Fiona's face paled, and she cleared her throat as she set her face into a neutral state. "Why do you ask?"

"Oh, I asked her about my brother, who I came here to find, but she was very weird about it. Then, when she was leaving-"

Fiona put her hand in the air to stop him. "Look. This is a different country; you need to be careful. Be very aware of your surroundings. You can't just walk around putting yourself out there, yeah?"

Brennan didn't understand and frowned. "I wasn't, I was just asking if she'd seen my brother."

"Trust me, watch your back."

"So you know her?"

Fiona laughed dryly. "Her? Things aren't what they seem. I will tell you more in the morning. Get some rest, and we can talk over breakfast."

With that, she ducked out of view, leaving Brennan standing on the stairs. She definitely knew something about Brianna, and it wasn't good. He thought about how Fiona said, "*her?* " in reference to Brianna as if there was a secret he didn't know. A dark truth.

What the hell had he gotten himself into?

Chapter 18

Under the bog, murky spirits stirred. I struggled to see at first, then I noticed eyes peering at me. They were red, green, and yellow, glowing like a flaming effigy. I saw many of them around, but I couldn't see what they were or how close they were to me. Reaching out, I felt to see if the space was enclosed, but the more I fished around, the more I realized I was certainly caught in a pond bed. The ground felt squishy, the muck squeezing between my toes. Somehow, I'd lost my shoes when I went under, the tendrils yanking me below into a deep chasm.

"Hello!"

I screamed several times, adjusting to my surroundings. Not underwater but under the surface all the same. I could see webs and abstract threads all over, feeling trapped inside a loom—a tapestry of gleaming, silken strings entangled around me.

"Who's there? I see your eyes, and I can feel you fuckers. You may think you can mess with me, you... you elves, but you can't. Eventually, the drugs will wear off, and I'll sober up. I've been here before. This isn't Carson's first trip around the sun, believe that shit."

Convinced the LSD was playing tricks on me, I let the cocaine snake its way into my brain—the two substances twisting my sanity. Together and apart at the same time. Forcing myself toward clarity, I tried to calm my nerves.

"Keep it together, Carson. Breathe. You are letting your anxiety get the best of you. Release the stress of Grandpa's death and Brennan's bullshit. Just breathe for fuck's sake. *Breathe.*" Flynn's words resonated in my mind.

The more my eyes adjusted to the darkness, the clearer I could see through the thick of it. Noticing an incline, it appeared to me that I sat in the center of the bog. As I peered around, I saw the middle of a bowl, and five pairs of glowing eyes gleaming at me from the circumference. I wondered why I couldn't see the rest of them, but there seemed to be an inky blob behind each set, moving around the bog with little form, taunting me.

A strange buzzing moved past my head. "Get the fuck away from me," I yelled, remembering I had a lighter in my pocket. I flicked the Zippo and watched the flame ignite, casting a low glow around me.

Beyond the small flare of amber were several shadows. They stretched across the pond, moving like worms.

"Shit!"

I looked at the elevation and ran toward it. My feet sank in the dense, wet mire. It felt like running through pig slop. Part of me wondered if I was stuck in a trough, the gunk around me immense and heavy. A muscular batch of goop rose with each footstep as if it contained life itself within the muck.

Halfway across the bog basin, I felt the beings wrap around me. "Fuck you, demons. You aren't real. You are only an extension of my thoughts and the drugs," I told myself, wrestling free.

Managing to slip past the shadow people, I ran closer to the edge of the bog, eyeing an escape. However, I was out of my element and out of sorts.

Further, I sank.

It made it difficult to wade through, but I managed—thigh-deep in scum, close to the edge of darkness. The moonlight trickled overhead, and the bit of lunar glow acted as a guide. The chaos inside me grew, and I inched closer, emerging from the bleak density.

"You fuckers can't touch me," I scoffed, dragging myself out of the bog, back onto the cool forest floor. My body trembled from exhaustion and fear.

I saw Flynn and cried out. "Help me, Flynn. I'm tripping too hard. You gotta talk me down from this. Bring me back to reality. I felt like I went under that thing, like I was in some bad place."

"Oh, but you are. You are where you belong, Carson. You are home," he replied flatly.

Suddenly, his eyes turned green, and he shape-shifted. In a moment's breath, Flynn grew demonic, his ears growing long and pointy. His beautiful face grew weathered, causing him to appear diseased and decayed, as if he were nothing but rot. Living death.

"Flynn, what the hell is happening to you?" I asked, mortified by the terrifying metamorphosis taking place before me, his skin white as a ghost as he continued to shift.

"I am Sidhe, and you are here to melt with me. To complete your destiny. Now it is time to return to where it is you came from."

Feeling the creature that was once Flynn tear at my abdomen, I screamed, my throat stretching into oblivion. In one swipe, the being's claws sliced my stomach open, the tearing unraveling my insides. They spilled, my intestines spewing from my gut as I collapsed.

"What the fuck are you?" I screamed in terror.

"I already told you, my dear Carson. God, you never listen, do you?"

My body grew flushed. I was dying, the end drawing near. I'd come all this way to Ireland to perish in the forests of Wicklow. Kicking on the ground for dear life, something moved around inside me. It wiggled and jerked, making me squeamish inside.

Whatever this thing was inside me, it was climbing out of my core, headfirst. Blood continued to pool below my body as I rolled on my back, sweaty, arching my anatomy in a twisted contortion. The hole in my gut grew bigger, and the head of the thing pushed out of my belly. Then I saw the antenna, panicking as it moved out of my skin.

What the fuck is happening to me?

"Your time has come. This is your fate, Carson," the spirit beside me whispered. No longer Flynn, the succubus preyed, dead set on devouring me.

"Why me?" I cried, my bones heating up.

"Again, *destiny*. Your family roots run deep, far down beneath the bog. There you will meet your end and your beginning. It is time, my child. Now go."

The creature inside me crawled from my brutalized frame, and I recognized it—a caterpillar. The larvae pulsated, luminous and vibrant, glowing green as it travelled from my body over to the Sidhe spirit guiding it, my skin an empty shell.

I was no longer me, but rather a caterpillar-human hybrid.

It seemed I no longer had control over my anatomy. I was being controlled and manipulated outside my will.

"You overdid it tonight," I bargained as I tried to rationalize the change happening to me. "It's only the drugs, it has to be. Too much acid and cocaine, add in the grief, and here we are."

The caterpillar me meandered its way closer to the bog, shimmering like a glow stick. It went near the edge of the water, then jumped in.

With no control over where my new form went, the spirits played me like an Irish fiddle.

Further into the bog, my little larval legs inched until I crawled back to the center of the bog.

The eyes appeared tenfold at first until there were a hundred dancing around me. The shadow figure stretched along the floor, wrapping its limbs around me. As that happened, I felt the threads on the base of the bog draw near, the webbing climbing closer, making me anxious about what was to come.

"Time to heat up," a voice said. "Liquid and bone will leave you alone. Liquid and bone, never going home."

Chapter 19

The sunlight streaming through the window hurt Brennan's eyes, and he rolled away from it, allowing his brain to absorb his current situation. Flashes of Brianna crossed his mind, and he frowned. What had Fiona said after he asked about the redheaded woman?

Things aren't what they seem.

He groaned and sat up, his body still not adjusted to the time change. His mouth tasted like a large rat had taken a shit in it, and he fumbled around the floor for his bag to retrieve his toothbrush.

As promised, there was a stack of towels and washcloths on the dresser. Brennan got up and retrieved them with the toothbrush clasped tightly in his fist. He'd forgotten toothpaste and hoped Fiona had a tube. The hallways were dimly lit, the windows at the end covered in dense curtains. The other bedrooms were closed, and Brennan wondered if there were other guests. Only one bathroom, so he'd make it quick just in case.

After a decent brushing of his teeth with a found tube of toothpaste, Brennan took off his clothes and turned on the shower. The pipes began to squeal and rattle as water coursed through them.

"Fuck," Brennan muttered, hoping he wasn't waking up the whole house.

The water was hot, and he forgot about his worries as he stepped in, letting the scalding stream make a river down his back. Steam surrounded him, and he sighed, allowing his muscles to relax. That was better. He scrubbed his hair with a bottle of what he hoped was shampoo, as the label was gone. It smelled like shampoo and lathered up, so he took his chances and used it to wash the rest of his body. He'd give Fiona a little extra money for using her supplies.

His eyes were clamped tight to prevent suds from running in them when he heard the door open slowly. He thought he'd locked it. Damnit.

"Hey, I'm in here. Sorry, I thought the door was locked. I'll be out in just a sec."

No answer came, and Brennan rinsed the soap off his face to open one of his eyes a slit. He was sure he'd heard the door. He peered out, and the door was cracked open a little. He glanced around the bathroom, confused. Had someone come in, then realized it was occupied and left?

He finished the shower and pushed the curtain back, still guarding his privates with the thin plastic. The bathroom was empty. Using one of the towels Fiona left for him, Brennan stepped out and wrapped the terry cloth fabric around his waist. He remembered locking the door. Did Fiona have a key? Surely she did, but why would she come in, then not say anything? He didn't know her, but it didn't seem like something she'd do to her guests.

Using another towel to scrub himself dry, he went to the mirror to wipe it so he could see himself. As he peered up into the mirror, he gasped. Words were written in the steam on the glass, and he knew for sure those weren't there before. Or had they been, and the steam made them apparent? Either way, the message scrawled across the mirror seemed to be just for him.

He is not here; he has never been. Go home and forget why you came.

If this was someone's idea of a joke, Brennan didn't find it the least bit funny. Was Brianna, or Fiona, trying to make him leave without finding Carson? Brianna, maybe, but Fiona had no dog in this fight. Brennan used a towel to erase the message, however, it began to reform as the steam danced across the surface. He yanked the bathroom door fully open to let the steam escape and watched as the message became nothing.

Fiona was in the kitchen when he came down, and Brennan waited for a moment for her to notice him in the doorway. She turned with a pan of some type of pastry and smiled at him, as if she'd known he was there all along.

"Sleep alright?" she asked and slid the baked goods into a basket lined with a tea towel.

Brennan nodded, making his way to a small table, and sat down. "Am I the only one staying here right now?"

Fiona cocked her head, her brow knitted. "You are at the moment. Why?"

"Oh, I thought someone came in the bathroom when I was taking a shower," he offered.

"No. No one is here. I've been cooking for the last hour or so. Maybe it was Dreadful."

Brennan recoiled. "I mean, it was weird, but I wouldn't call it dreadful."

Fiona began to laugh, then pointed to a gray cat sitting on the windowsill. "Sorry, no. My cat's name is Dreadful. She likes to explore."

Brennan felt silly for a moment and watched the cat grooming itself with no interest in his presence. Maybe the cat had come in, but he was sure he'd locked the door, and cats don't write. "Is it just you running this place? You don't have any help?"

Fiona picked up the basket of pastries and a French press of coffee. "Follow me, we can sit on the back porch to eat. Here, will you grab the butter dish?"

Brennan saw the cow-shaped dish on the table and picked it up. He followed Fiona out to the porch, which overlooked a small garden. Fiona already had plates for them and dishes of eggs and ham. She set the pastries down and eyed him. "Probably more food than we can eat, but I like to cook."

Brennan sat down and began heaping food on his plate. He could make a solid dent in the spread. "So? You do this all alone? No husband?"

Fiona pulled and chair out across from him, her eyes never leaving his face as she twisted her dark hair off her neck to her back. "No husband. I don't swing that way. No wife, either. Only me and the cat. Why do you ask?"

Not wanting to put her on guard, Brennan shrugged and scooped eggs into his mouth. She certainly knew how to cook. "No reason, I guess. Seems like a lot to handle for one person. You do all the cleaning, cooking, everything?"

"I do. I prefer it that way. No one to do it wrong the first time. I'm a bit of a control freak, I suppose."

That answered a lot of questions Brennan had that he didn't say. It was only he and Fiona in the house. Well, and Dreadful. He didn't think Fiona would write that message. His thoughts went back to Brianna. "Do you believe in ghosts?"

Fiona stopped with her fork in midair. "Sure. These old places have had many people over the years. Some are bound to stick around."

Brennan considered his next question carefully, not wanting her to think he was off his rocker. "Is Brianna, the lady from last night, a ghost?"

At that, Fiona set her fork down. She shook her head. "I guess now is a better time than any other, yeah? No, she's not a ghost. She's not even really a *she* in a way. What do you know about our folklore?"

Folklore? "You mean like leprechauns and fairies?" Brennan asked.

"Not like the American version, no. You all make it seem light-hearted and fun. We don't feck with that shite here. Your version is cute. Ours is much more sinister."

"Are you saying Brianna is some kind of creature or something?" Brennan inquired, now thinking maybe Fiona was off her rocker.

"Something like that. What you call fairies or Fae is French and English evolved from what we call Sidhe or Aos Sí. They are not happy little sprites that flit through the woods and sniff flowers. They are creatures with their own intent. Not always well-intentioned, mind you. Honestly, they are pretty dangerous beings."

Brennan focused on his food, to not let his face show his doubt. He wanted to push back, but things were too strange not to hear her out. "So you are saying the woman I met last night is Fa-, uh, whatever you called it? She looked like a regular lady."

Until she didn't.

Fiona leaned forward and put her hand over his. "I'm not telling you anything more than our folklore. Remember, you came to me on this journey. You need to come to any conclusions on your own. You tell me what you believe, yeah?"

Brennan met her eyes, and everything in his body felt like it was trying to turn inside out to escape his skin. She didn't blink, and he couldn't either. All of a sudden, something about his grandmother made more sense to him than it ever had. The visions of the face above him when he tried to sleep. His odd cravings and always feeling like he wasn't part of the world he was brought into. How he couldn't even reconcile with the human aspects of himself. Every fiber of his being was screaming to pay attention and accept the truth.

About his grandmother, about his father, and what they did. His mother and sister. About his grandfather. About himself. Their history, their destiny.

About Carson.

He shook his head. "My brother is gone, isn't he?"

Chapter 20

My body ached all the way down to the bone. My skin burned, and the heat within me engulfed my flaming core. Darkness plagued my soul, my past pinning me to the earth. This was my destiny, my rite, a passage, a shift into the spirit world. All my life, I knew this time would come, more than human, and part of the bog.

Hearing the voices all around me, my life withered away. In the black, the cosmos called my name. No longer me as I recognized myself. I moved like a caterpillar, slowly preparing for rebirth.

Voices permeated the air, hypnotic, distorted, and luring. They sounded terrifying, making demands and predicting my demise. "We want to see you die. We want to see you reborn," they told me in repetitive, unearthly chants. Over and over, they sang like a ghostly choir. "We want to see you die, we want to see you reborn."

Shaking, I curled into a ball, the heat growing increasingly unbearable. My hair crumbled, turning to dead leaves as all the strands fell from my scalp, reminding me of a Christmas tree at the end of the holiday season. The thought triggered more memories, and I felt like two people at once. A memory I'd forgotten surfaced.

I saw myself as a teen, my father hitting me with a belt at my grandmother's command, my ass raw, the red of my skin matching my father's festive sweater. It started as slapping, then turned to the oak switch, hitting my back over and over. The lacerations ran deep, and my flesh cried, breaking under the pressure of the sharp twig.

It hurt like hell.

Being whipped is the most horrific pain. I wouldn't wish it on my worst enemy, and trust me, I don't. I'm not that kind of person, not like my father. After what I've been through, I'm an empath, and this process I'm enduring only solidifies my point.

Watching my dad whip me, my back bleeding with a hundred lashings, I sobbed, terrified, broken, eviscerated, and abandoned. Becoming a part of the bog now, more memories flooded my mind.

The beating continued.

My grandma grinned from ear to ear as I cried. "There's no mercy for boys like you," she whispered through thin lips, enjoying my torment.

"Stop, please," I begged, passing out from the agony.

When I awoke that night, I lay in a puddle of blood, piss dripping down my leg. I smelled of shit and disgust. I can no longer remember what I even did to receive such a punishment.

I rarely did.

More nightmares washed over me. The next one plagued me from my college days. I staggered around a buddy's house, drunk at a party, smoking crack with friends. All of a sudden, they shifted into creatures with red eyes and dark wings. I thought I was having some kind of acid flashback from the week prior. The heat raged inside me. It felt like burning in an oven on broil, my skin charring. I couldn't hold it in anymore; I needed to scream.

"Help! Heeeeeeeelp me! Help! Somebody, please. I'm begging you. Stop, this is torture, this is Hell," I cried, shrinking.

I tightened my legs and felt my knees, or whatever they were now, press against my chin. It was then that I realized I was cooking from the inside out. The hottest part of my anatomy burned in my bones. The calcium in them separated as they transformed to mush. Resembling marshmallows, they felt sticky and scalding. My blood boiled and my organs melted, turning to soup. For hours, my bones stewed, slowly becoming goo.

"You won't survive this, you're not meant to," a voice called out.

"Grandma?" I shouted, tasting iron in my throat. Blood and bile spewed from my mouth as I clenched my throat.

"Liquid and bone."

The words triggered more fire. The flames burning within continued, consuming me as I wept. Lying there in a ball, bald and on fire, I welcomed death.

IT WAS THANKSGIVING 1980, and Brennan and I were at odds with each other. Drunk and on blow, I lashed out, acting like a real piece of shit. He desperately tried to play the better brother, making an effort to calm me down.

"You're not mad at me, you're mad at Dad," he told me. "Let's go for a ride."

Climbing into his brand-new car, Brennan jingled his keys. "Come on. We'll pump some tunes and cruise the streets like old times."

"Fine," I agreed, lighting a cigarette as I slid into the car and put my seatbelt on. "Drive slow, though. It's Thanksgiving, and you know the pigs are out."

"I'll take it slow," Brennan assured me. "Trust me."

Peeling out of the driveway, we headed down back streets. We passed a joint back and forth, chatting and enjoying each other's company. We'd completely forgotten about the fight. I remember looking out the window, watching the trees flicker by. Then, something peculiar caught my eye: a winged creature. At first, I figured I was stoned, but the more I focused on its form, the more I saw it for what it was.

It hovered over us, following the sports car as it sped down the road. Brennan paid no mind, unaware of the inky blob stalking the vehicle. I could feel it feeding me messages and caught glimpses of its eyes as it flew. Mesmerizing, hypnotic, and seductive, if not for the painful pitch radiating in my ears, crippling my anatomy, I would have found it intriguing.

Foam leaked from my mouth, my muscles contracting, as I felt my body scald. Everything burned: my skin, hair, head, and extremities. Time distorted, slowing to a standstill. I tried to turn to Brennan, but I couldn't. The spirit traveling above us had me paralyzed. It felt like a thousand felines had scratched my skin and eyeballs. Their nails dug into my retinas, squashing my eyeballs into a milky slop.

Convulsing, I heard Brennan screaming bloody murder. He could no longer move his body, frozen like me. The car accelerated, the engine purring as the dark entity sped the vehicle down the desolate country road, zig-zagging over the yellow line like a sidewinder snake.

We both shouted, but we couldn't hear one another. The translucent demon flying overhead hissed, ready to orchestrate an elaborate crash. We both braced for impact as we saw the elm ahead. Before the collision, I saw its face stretching far and wide, eyes beaming with anger. It laughed, seeing the fear in our eyes. I don't know what saved us that night. Maybe the evil shadow beings planned this all, and it was only a fear tactic, a way to intimidate us. To break our spirits.

We just missed the tree, swerving off the road and into a muddy cornfield. The muck provided traction, slowing us to a halt. Still unable to move, we both saw the being shatter the windshield, reach into the car, yank us out of the vehicle, and drag us across the field.

I can still feel the mud on my face and taste the grit in my teeth. That... thing, it pulled us through the depths of Hell as we begged for salvation.

Fortunately, that night, it came.

Chapter 21

The conversation with Fiona over breakfast stuck in Brennan's mind. She wasn't one to get caught up in fanciful theories, so he took her words seriously. When he asked about Carson, she met his eyes and asked one simple question.

"Do you think Carson is gone?"

The problem was, Brennan did. Every cell in his being was telling him Carson no longer existed. Yet a lingering sensation told him they were still connected, so Carson couldn't be dead. He didn't know how to explain it, but it was like Carson was both gone and there at the same time. It was something to hold onto, at least.

"I don't know," Brennan responded.

Fiona took a bite of her food and shrugged, keeping locked on his eyes. "I think you do."

They finished breakfast, and Brennan helped with the cleanup afterward. Dreadful, all of a sudden, took notice of Brennan and began rubbing against him as he dried the dishes Fiona was washing.

She side-eyed the cat and grinned. “Looks like she has bestowed her grace upon you.”

“What?” Brennan asked, confused.

“Dreadful. She likes you. For now, anyway,” Fiona explained, gesturing toward the oddly affectionate cat. “Do you want to take a drive after we are done here? I can show you the countryside.”

Brennan frowned. If Fiona hadn’t made it clear she wasn’t into guys, he’d think she was hitting on him. She rinsed her hands off, then dried them on a towel. Dreadful jumped off the counter and followed Fiona out of the kitchen into the front hall. Brennan hung the towel he was using to dry dishes on the faucet and trailed behind.

Fiona grabbed her purse and jingled her keys at him with a grin. “Yeah?”

Brennan smiled. “Sure, sounds fun. Any chance you might have an idea on how I can track my brother down while we are at it?”

“You said he likes to party? There’s a house outside of town that a lot of the boys like to hang out at. We can take a drive out there and see if anyone recognizes your brother. They are a rowdy lot, but nothing to worry about.”

Brennan grabbed his things in case he decided not to come back with Fiona after the drive. If he found any trace of Carson, he was going to follow it. He had the sensation he was running out of time. That *Carson* was running out of time. If he hadn't already.

Fiona kissed Dreadful on the head and held the door for Brennan to go out. Behind him, she locked the door and gave it a jiggle for posterity. Brennan waited for her by the gate, then followed her to the car. Fiona moved differently from most women he knew. She was comfortable in her skin in a way that reminded him of Desiree, and it made him homesick for maybe the first time ever.

They were quiet on the drive out of town, and Brennan felt an odd sense of déjà vu when they hit the countryside. Like he'd been there before, but he knew he hadn't. Yet he could almost pinpoint the turns they were going to take before Fiona even put on her blinker. Maybe he was channeling Carson on some level. Maybe his twin *had* come out that way.

When he saw the old house in the distance, he knew it was the house Fiona referred to, and Carson had indeed gone out there. He didn't know why, but he could see it as clear as day. He pointed at the structure.

"My brother was here."

Fiona cocked her head, a small grin on her lips. "Is this a twin thing?"

"I guess so. We don't really do that, but I know he was here. I can feel it."

Fiona turned up the driveway to the house. "Well, either way, this is the house I was talking about, so you must be onto something."

The house was run down and littered with bottles and garbage as if it were in a constant state of parties. A large, shaggy dog ran off the porch to greet them, its tail wagging despite its ferocious warning. Brennan hesitated getting out of the car, not sure if the dog would go after him.

Fiona shook her head. "That's Buster. He's all noise and fur. He doesn't bite."

Brennan wondered about Fiona's connection to the people who hung out at the house, as she clearly knew a lot about them and their dog. He pushed the door open, and Buster ran over to him, slobbering and licking him. "Uh, hi, boy. Let me out, Buster."

The front door opened, and a striking young man stepped out. His hair was white, and he was smoking a cigarette, peering at them with almost black eyes. Fiona raised a hand at the man, and he gestured back with a slight lift of his chin. His eyes never left Brennan.

"What are you doing out this way, Fi?" the man asked, familiar with her.

"Aye, Patrick, my boarder here is looking for his brother who may have come out here," Fiona called back, motioning to Brennan with a flick of her hand.

"That's right? Why do you think he was all the way out here, like?" Patrick asked smugly, clearly not want to share any information.

Fiona rolled her eyes. "Don't pull that with me, Patrick. He's a partier, and word in town has it he came out here to let loose."

Brennan hid his expression by pretending to appreciate the landscape. There was no word in town, but Fiona seemed to know what she was doing. The man leaned against the door jamb and flicked his cigarette into the yard. Buster ran at it, sniffed the discarded butt, then trotted off, disinterested.

"Alright, then. Come on in."

Fiona led the way, following Patrick's slender frame through the door. The house was messy, and people were still sleeping in different areas. Patrick waved his hand around. "Take a look, boy. Maybe he's here somewhere."

Brennan could sense that Carson wasn't, but didn't want to piss off Patrick, who could send him packing. He walked through the rooms, glancing at the different sleeping and passed-out forms. None was Carson, as he suspected. He came back out from one of the bedrooms and shook his head. Fiona and Patrick were talking in hushed tones and stopped when Brennan came back. He felt like they were keeping something from him.

"Do you get a lot of Americans out here to party?" Brennan asked Patrick, tired of the bullshit.

Patrick shrugged. "Sometimes, yeah."

Brennan was at his wits' end and headed for the front door. "Dude, if you're going to be a dick about it, I'll go look for myself."

Realizing Brennan was serious, Fiona went toward him and put her hand on his arm. "Wait. Patrick can be a pain in the ass, but slow down. Don't you have a picture of your brother?"

Brennan swallowed his anger and pulled out a folded photograph. "Yeah. This is Carson. We are twins, but don't look alike."

He handed the picture to Fiona, who brought it over to Patrick. At first, Patrick barely glanced at the photo, but then something in it caught his eye, and he took the picture, looking closer at it. The color drained from his already pale face as he met Fiona's eyes. A silent message passed between them as she turned to Brennan, her eyes wide.

Brennan stared at the two, who seemed to have lost their voices. "What? Have you seen him or not?"

"Aye," Patrick whispered and handed the picture back to Brennan. "I've seen him. You Americans come here thinking we are all jovial and shite. A fun vacation to trace your roots and take home some souvenirs."

Brennan was thoroughly confused by Patrick's shift and accusations. What did any of that have to do with his brother? He slid the photo back into his pocket and looked at Patrick for clarity. "You have seen Carson? When? Is he here? Where did he go?"

Patrick broke eye contact and dropped his head, whispering something that sounded like Flynn to Fiona. Brennan strained to hear what he was saying, but Fiona's expression set him on guard. What the hell was going on?

Fiona came over and grabbed Brennan's arm, dragging him out of the house. He resisted, wanting to know what Patrick was saying. He pulled away, ready to fight, and was shocked when Fiona reached out and slapped him.

"What the hell?" Brennan yelled, touching his stinging face. "What is going on, Fiona?"

Her eyes blazed, and she leaned close. "Your brother was here, but he left with another person."

"Who? Brianna?"

Fiona looked away. "No. Worse."

Worse? What had Carson gotten himself into? Brennan saw Patrick watching them from the doorway; this time, he appeared more afraid than anything else. Brennan faced Fiona again, his head tipped.

"Fiona, please, tell me what is happening? Where is Carson? Who did he leave with?"

"Flynn," was all she said as if that should mean something to him. It didn't.

"Who is Flynn? Is Carson still with him?"

Fiona shook her head as if she couldn't remember something, then looked up, her eyes distant. "We should certainly hope he isn't."

"Why? What are you trying to say? I don't understand what is going on. If he's with this Flynn, what does that mean?" Brennan asked desperately.

"Your brother is in terrible danger. *If* he's still alive."

Chapter 22

When we were ten years old, Brennan began to have what we called "episodes" at night. Occurring every week, and occasionally several times a month, I'd usually wake up to him mumbling incoherently. His speech would be muffled, but as the minutes passed, it grew louder and more boisterous. He'd say things like, "It's inevitable. Your time will come."

This particular night in fifth grade, I lay in bed sick with the flu. I'd been bedridden for two days, and Brennan was lonely. Without me to play with, he moped around the house before taking a walk by himself to the river. He was gone for a while but eventually came back crying, claiming a boy he'd met shape-shifted into an old woman before his eyes. He said she was haggard, her ears reminiscent of an elf. A demonic elf. The same could be said for her jagged teeth, he swore.

"She grabbed my arm and tried to pull me into the river with her," he insisted.

Father called him a "sissy boy" and gave him the belt for making up stories. Later that evening, Brennan's next episode became like no other before. We were both asleep, and I lay on my back with Brennan in the bed next to mine. At first, he grumbled, minor moans mixed with quiet humming. Over time, it turned to gibberish, then ritualistic speaking.

I could tell it was a specific call or chant, maybe pagan or Celtic in origin. I recognized some of the words from an old Druid book I'd found at the library in town. At the time, we were both interested in magic, Wicca, and Irish folklore, so it didn't sound foreign to me. We were odd children with strange interests and tendencies, and this experience was no exception.

The chants turned to singing.

"One of you will burn, one of you will melt," he sang over and over.

Then, all of a sudden, Brennan started thrashing, his arms pinned to the bed as if something was holding him down. I wanted to get up, to help, but I couldn't. Too ill to intervene, my mind and body were stuck in a fever dream. The only reason I know this story was true is that our father saw the whole thing. Even he acted concerned that night. He seemed to be aware of something we weren't, and it was making him afraid.

Turning my head slightly, I saw my brother spitting foam from his mouth, his neck jerking side to side as if he was possessed. He twitched and seethed, his eyes crossed while he spat. "Burn!" he screamed. That's when our father came into the room.

"Lucifer!" he shouted, observing his son battling a demon we couldn't see but could feel all around us.

Brennan's back arched unnaturally, his wrists turning and twisting like the limbs of a tree. Then I heard his pinky break, wincing at the cracking.

His body undulated, convulsing the whole way down. My father made no effort to rescue my brother and seemed almost to expect the encounter. I watched helplessly from my bed, wondering why my father wasn't intervening. He looked to be almost in a trance.

Floating above the mattress, Brennan appeared peaceful, hanging near the ceiling. His face sat only inches from the wood beams, his back a full seven feet from the bed. When he plummeted to the sheets, our father thanked God, leaving the room without checking on Brennan.

My body was depleted, as my fever reached 103 degrees. I thought I'd certainly die that night, especially when the entity entered the room and tortured me. The creature stood there, inky and stretching like the limbs of an elm tree. Although its body was light and airy, it weighed a ton, crushing me with each breath the damn thing took. When I saw its red eyes sucking at my soul, I knew it was real.

That night, our childhood was lost.

The being grabbed me by my shirt, heaving me across the room, my legs kicking as the rug scuffed my knees. Brennan lay paralyzed by fear, still processing his possession. I couldn't yell or beg for mercy, only succumb and allow this creature to pull me around the room like a rag doll. My toes curled, and I spewed foam as the dark entity dragged me across the floor. Our father never returned to our room that night. He left us to fend for ourselves.

Ever since that night, every time I get the flu, that demonic fucker comes back, yanking me by my hair and taking me under my bed, far below the ground.

It is there, in the underworld, I see that thing for what it is. A dreaded spirit sent from the darkest depths of Hell to devour me, and now that demon is staring me in the face. There is no escaping this time.

With my body crammed in the muck, my feet gnawed by spiders, I picked at my remaining self. Mostly a thick, gelatinous slop at this point, I bore hardly any form at all. Even where my fingers and toes should have been, there existed only strange, wiggling, worm-like appendages.

It hurts.

It burns and aches.

It's turned me to mush. Now, as I boil, my entire anatomy scalding, I realize what is happening to me. I'm undergoing some sort of metamorphosis.

I'm in a cocoon, deep beneath the bog, transforming. This is my destiny, my calling, my journey. I wish Brennan were here with me to undergo this process of rebirth, but he isn't, and now I don't know if I'll ever see him again. Flashes of our childhood emerge from the farthest corners of my soul, and everything in me shifted.

The agony.

The pain.

I want it to end—all of it, each and every part of it. I want to see myself as a person again, not this boiling liquid crystalizing inside a cocoon. I want life again, not death.

Give me light and let me live.

The creature appeared in sickness and during every solstice. That consistency terrified me, and I came to expect it. Every autumn, I dreaded the start of winter because I knew the entity lurked, waiting to torture me.

To feed off me.

Two solstices ago, when the shapeshifting creature surfaced, I worked at the moor—a late-night shift to finish a boat restoration project. Heading home for the night, I strolled along the pier, away from the moor, when something put its arm around me. It felt like a person walking beside me, holding me tight. In one swift motion, the demon slung me into the cold ocean, my body sinking into the icy sea. Drifting under the saltwater, I saw it staring at me, face to face.

"Liquid and bone," the voice whispered, holding me down below the surface.

Gasping for air, my mouth filled with ocean water, and I choked on the Atlantic, fearing death yet again, an endless cycle I could never escape. Yet, it never let me die. It would bring me to the brink, then let me go. A sick game I could never win.

Fighting for my life, tangled in seaweed, I slowly breached the surface. Sucking in oxygen, I welcomed the freezing night air on my face and climbed onto the pier. Soaked and bitterly cold, my body shook from fear and the frigid temperatures. My heartbeat slowed, and my body played tricks on me, heating up as I stripped off my clothes. I was falling into hypothermia, and the spirit was taunting me, laughing at my terror.

One of my coworkers saw me shivering out on the pier and called for help. Eventually, the paramedics rushed me to the hospital, and I spent the night in the ICU. By morning, I was myself again, but Brennan still drove two hours to come see me. I was so thankful, then. Now, I really needed him. More than ever. He wouldn't be able to help me, however.

No one could.

My flesh tore from my body, ripping from my taint, across my abdomen and back, up over my shoulders and knees. A rupture in my throat caused my esophagus to collapse, my neck snapping, drooping to one side. Feces leaked from my anus, spilling, rushing out of me. My testicles shrank, and my cock veins burst. Watching my genitals melt away, my ass screamed like a banshee as my stomach burst, my organs popping, sizzling, and broiling similar to a well-cooked lasagna.

My eyes ached, and my nose dripped from my face, reminiscent of a Salvador Dali painting. I imagined myself as candle wax, oozing in the Sahara, my scalp splitting, my brain bleeding, seizing, cooking like a baked cinnamon roll. Feeling my guts stew, my skin peeled away, then turned to soup, my bones following suit. Entirely liquid, my body was now the chrysalis consuming me.

I was no longer aware of myself or who I was in my past life; all I understood was my transformation, and now it was time to cool and begin the process of rapid cell division. I heard a voice tell me I needed to increase the number of cells in my body from fifty to over fifty thousand. I didn't know what that meant, but I could feel my consciousness following orders on autopilot.

Slowly, my eyes, wings, and antennae took shape, materializing all around me. Wrapped tightly like a joint, I felt my anatomy form. Then I heard a voice whisper, "The chrysalis is the way out."

"Liquid and bone, never goin' home."

The words seemed to come from nowhere, yet everywhere. Spirits enveloped me, the space dimming with each breath. Submerged in darkness, I wanted to die. The pain continued to engulf me. I was a blob of chaos screaming into an endless abyss with no one to hear me. I missed my brother, I missed my family. Alone, and dying a miserable death, I hope the new cells filling my new body will guide me to be reborn. If I failed my transformation, that meant the evil spirits had won, and my end was near.

Liquid and bone, never goin' home.

Chapter 23

Brennan ran out into the nearby field, his heart beating a million miles a minute. He didn't know what he was doing, but something told him to go in that direction. As his lungs burned, he bent over to catch his breath. Fiona caught up with him, clearly not as out of shape as he was.

"What are you doing, Brennan?" she asked, coming closer to him. "Why did you run out here?"

He shook his head, and he stood back up, gazing around the area. "I have no fucking clue. I panicked."

Fiona watched him, her eyes tired. "Well, at least you went the right direction, even if you didn't mean to."

"What do you mean?'

"Patrick said Flynn and Carson headed off this way. Toward the bog," she explained.

"The bog? What's there?" Brennan asked.

"A bog. Nothing else, really. Apparently, they wanted to be alone. That guy Flynn? He has a place out there, word has it he and Carson left the party and went to Flynn's."

Brennan peered off into the distance and started walking in the direction his soul felt called. Maybe he and Carson did have the twin thing, after all. Fiona caught up to him and grabbed his arm. Brennan yanked his arm away. "I need to find my brother."

"I know, why are you walking away?" Fiona asked, confused.

"You said Flynn's place was out this way, right? I'm going to find it."

Fiona laughed. "Alright? It's like twenty or so miles away by car, so it may take you a bit, yeah?"

Brennan paused and rubbed his face. "Damnit. I guess I thought you meant they walked over there."

Fiona shook her head. "Not likely. Do you want to take my car? I can give you a ride, though no one seems to know where exactly Flynn lives."

"Of course they don't," Brennan muttered. "No wonder my family moved to America."

If Fiona took offense, she didn't show it. She knew Brennan was stressed about his brother being missing, and now with someone who might be a danger to him. "Tell me about your family, other than Carson. When did they leave Ireland?"

Brennan chewed his lip as they headed back to Fiona's car. "My grandparents were born here, but they said their family disapproved of their marriage, so they moved to the States when they were young. Really, my grandmother's family disapproved. My grandfather doesn't remember his family. Said he was an orphan or something like that. Anyway, they wanted a fresh start and moved to America."

"Clearly, they had children since you are here. How many children did they have?" Fiona inquired, fishing her keys out of her bag.

"Just my father."

"Ah, I see, and your father and mother had only you and Carson?"

Brennan paused, the memories flooding painfully back. He didn't want to think about them right now; he needed to stay focused. "More or less."

"More or less. So more? Or less?" Fiona wasn't going to let it drop.

"More. My mother died giving birth to my sister, who also died."

Fiona stared at him, her brow furrowed with concern. "I'm so sorry, Brennan. That's horrible. I feel like nowadays that almost never occurs."

"I guess it still happens. Well..." Now he doubted that was what occurred, after having visions of his father and grandmother killing his sister and mother.

"Well? Was it something else?"

"I don't know. I saw something. I had this, I guess, image of my grandmother murdering my baby sister right after she was born. Then making my father kill my mother as she cried out for her newborn daughter. I don't know. It could be shit in my head."

Fiona put her hand on his arm. "Your grandfather? Where was he?"

Brennan shook his head. "I have no idea. Honestly, all of this was just a story I heard until I had the vision of it."

"I see. Both of your grandparents were born here in Ireland?" Fiona asked, opening the car door.

"Yeah."

"O'Leary? That's a pretty common name around here, like. Do you know what your grandmother's maiden name was?"

Brennan didn't and wasn't sure why it mattered. "No, she never talked about her side of the family. I always assumed they had a falling out since they didn't approve of my grandfather."

He climbed into the car, and Fiona turned the key, bringing the engine to life. She turned around in the dirt driveway and headed back out toward the road. They drove in silence for a bit, then Fiona slowed the car and pointed across a field. "The bogs are out this way. Patrick said Flynn's place is out there."

"How do you know all of them?" Brennan asked, sensing she wasn't telling him everything.

Fiona kept her eyes on the road when she answered. "I did my fair share of craic back in the day. Probably more than my fair share. Most of those kids are younger than me, but it runs in generations. I knew their parents, partied with them. I remember some of those guys from when they were little, toddling around parties they never should have been at. I guess it was natural that they stayed after their parents moved on or died. I was done after I realized I was only bleeding myself dry and watching everyone I know disintegrate, so to speak."

Fiona was such a calm presence; Brennan had a hard time believing she'd ever been a party girl. She definitely had a few years on him from what he could tell. She seemed like someone's cool aunt, not a fucked up female version of Carson. Then again, Brennan had his secrets and wasn't one to judge anyone else's past. Or present.

"Did you know Flynn?" Brennan asked.

Fiona glanced at him, her eyes clouded, then gritted her teeth. "No one knows Flynn."

"What do you mean?"

"Flynn is like Brianna. They show up on the scene with no history, no family, no connections to anyone."

Brennan knew people like that back home and didn't think it was a big deal. People were transient, and a lot of people didn't have good relationships with their families. Himself included. "Yeah? Is that a problem?"

Fiona laughed. "Is that a problem? In one word, yes. Ireland is a small country. Of course, people come and go, and outsiders sometimes come in, but this is different. These are people *from* here, but also not. Maybe not even people."

Brennan was thoroughly confused. People who may or may not be people who were from there but weren't. It was some kind of fucking riddle he couldn't solve. "Explain it to me like I'm stupid."

Chuckling, Fiona raised an eyebrow. "That should be easy enough. Sometimes these, em, beings let's call them, show up. They look and talk like us, but no one knows them, yeah? We should, we all went to school together, our families know one another. However, these beings appear and integrate as if they have always been there, but they haven't, see? I know this doesn't make sense to you, but trust me when I tell you to be very careful and pay attention to your surroundings."

Brennan sighed. "Fiona, it's like you are speaking in tongues. If these aren't people and no one knows them, what the hell are they?"

"Sidhe."

"Oh, like fairies?"

"Remember what I told you before. This isn't anything Americans understand. It has been twisted and sanitized into something almost pleasant, endearing. They're not. Think more like demons or imps, although even those have been molded into something cute. These beings are ill-intentioned, spiteful, and malicious. Their goal is to mess things up. To fuck people over."

"So you think Brianna and Flynn are Sidhe?" Brennan asked, not sure he believed what she was saying, yet needing to know more.

"I know they are. So does Patrick. I imagine a lot of those boys back there know what Flynn is."

"Okay, so say you're right. Why would anyone hang out with them if that's true? Wouldn't they be petrified of malevolent spirits?"

Fiona nodded, then slowed the car to a stop. "Think about it this way, yeah? You know the saying, *keep your friends close, but your enemies closer*?"

"Yes?"

"That's why. They exist, and pretending they don't only allows them in. If we are aware and permit them to hang about, we can keep an eye on them."

"Fair enough. How can you tell if one is or isn't a Sidhe?" Brennan questioned. Until he saw Brianna shift in the light, he never would have guessed she wasn't just some pretty Irish girl.

"You can't. Not unless they show themselves. Many of us have been tricked. Some of us have paid the price," Fiona explained, shaking her head as if she knew personally.

"What do you mean by 'paid the price'?"

Fiona glanced out the window, an expression he couldn't quite place crossing her face. She met his eyes. "I am going to show you something. This is how I learned my lesson. Don't freak out."

Brennan tipped his head as she lifted her shirt to show her stomach. Deep, angry purple scars ran from under her breasts to below her pants waist line. It looked like a giant claw had tried to rip her open and was pretty damn successful in the process.

He frowned in confusion as he fixated on the gnarly marks. Whatever happened, it must have almost killed her. "My God. I don't understand, Fiona. What the fuck did that do to you?"

"Brianna."

Chapter 24

Being liquid is strange, but being boiling muck is even weirder. In this state, you're no longer a lifeform, really, but rather in between phases. Lost in a chrysalis of my own making, I unraveled, and now, after the intense cooling stage, I began to take a new form.

Damnit, Brennan. How could you? I thought to myself. At this point, everything became purely thought, but my inner monologue felt like a vibration, confusing me even further. I wasn't sure if I was communicating with myself, as it seemed like there were two of me. Or none of me. I couldn't make it make sense.

Encased in my new developing structure, I didn't recognize myself. Here, in this new state, paranoia stretched across my anatomy, making me cold.

Brennan. He turned on me. He did this time. My own brother, my own flesh and blood, the person I thought un-

derstood me more than anyone. I bet it was him who killed our mother. He forced his way into the womb, devouring her and taking me with him. Look, it makes perfect sense.

Here I am, trapped, molding, becoming something I'm not. He wanted me out of the picture; he wanted me dead. The spirit in me knew this and needed to change to adapt to his demands. What a fool I am. Since in utero, since birth and every aspect of life, he's tainted me, turned me rancid. Now look at me? Death. Rebirth. Life and the unknown? Who knows what's next? All I see is blackness... and where's my twin? Nowhere to be seen.

Convinced Brennan tricked me and led me to Ireland to die, I welcomed the metamorphosis. Time elapsed, and the heat in my being vanished more and more until I was cold, and my eyes and wings were fastening to the rest of my new body. Feeling the antenna protruding from my head, I panicked. No longer formless, but in a different configuration I couldn't relate to.

I don't want to be a butterfly. I don't want to be an insect. Please, somebody, help me! I'm not a bug, I'm not some spindly, winged being that lives a short life span, I'm human. I am a person with bones, blood, flesh, and organs. I have teeth, hair, and a nose. I have an abdomen and a belly button from the umbilical cord at birth, the one that made me separate from my brother. In the womb, I had my own sac, my own space, my own cord, and my own placenta. We didn't share. When did we ever?

Here's my last words: Brennan is a leech.

In an instant, everything in the chrysalis shifted, throwing me asunder. It began to pulse, expanding, morphing, and vibrating like an instrument. Unable to move my form to protect myself, I curled into myself to lessen the pressure on my fragile new existence.

Voices surrounded me.

Hearing the whispers, I fell into an empty space, my body evaporating as everything changed. My insect form dissolved, and a fresh type of human being began to emerge.

THE CHRYSALIS FLOATED BENEATH the bog, similar to a submarine lost at sea. Carson disappeared, no longer the man he once was. A different person, a new body, a being, an erected structure taking shape. His mind separated and melded into the chrysalis as it gently ascended. Forest debris caught in the bottom of the bog bed, mixed with murky water, created a quilt of gunk around him.

Fish, tadpoles, frogs, and tiny organisms drifted by the chrysalis. An obscure green light emitted from its intricate construction. The glow lit up the bog, blinding any amphibians in sight.

Oozing a peculiar substance, the chrysalis traveled further until it breached the surface. A dead tree caught under it lifted alongside the chrysalis, acting as hands pushing the vessel out of the bog.

Inside, Carson slowly rearranged, however, it wasn't pleasant. The pressure inside the chrysalis grew immense, causing Carson's current self to scream from its new belly. Carson wasn't quite a human yet, stuck between bug and plasma. This didn't mean he couldn't feel pain or emotion. Carson O'Leary could.

The agony.

The pain and dark spirits. How do they do this to me? Harass me, and torture me? Since birth, since childhood, since my adolescent years, oh, the horror. Something's been feeding off me, and the only thing I can think of is Brennan. What I thought was brotherly love was actually a sadistic game to take my life from me.

This is it. This is the end.

Carson felt claws and talons reaching into his new frame, tearing him into oblivion. In the darkness, Carson saw Brennan's unborn baby girl.

Carson heard the child's whispers, her desperate cries for help. The baby fought, trapped in an entanglement of vines and inky limbs. Carson could see glowing eyes leering at him; they were demonic and vile, ready to suck the life out of Brennan's child, making sure the girl never took a breath of oxygen. Like their baby sister.

"She will die," an evil-voiced said. "This is what she deserves. It is only fair for what you have done."

Confused, Carson continued to morph and shift, feeling the unborn child's fear. It was crippling, only adding to the terror inside him.

The fetus struggled, wading in darkness. Carson grew more self-aware, becoming claustrophobic in the chrysalis. He had hands and legs now, his head and mouth slowly taking shape. Unfamiliar, yet welcoming.

Spirits hijacked the vessel, tormenting Carson, filling the space with morbid images. The entities revealed their sinister qualities with Flynn taking shape in the chrysalis.

"Hello, Carson. Do you see? Do you see how your family has become a plague? Your roots are bruised, blackened, and wretched, much like your soul. Come with me, my love, and let's journey into the dark world together."

Carson tried to pull away, but couldn't, Flynn's power moving much too strongly. The entities surrounding the bog wanted the O'Leary men dead. No, not only the men. Their sister. Their mother. They were all being punished, and for what? He didn't know. Although Carson evolved, it wasn't enough to save him.

They wanted him, and they wanted him with them forever.

Battling the demons and struggling to make sense of reality, Carson O'Leary saw their grandfather. Old and grey, his skin wrinkled like a sundried apricot. Smiling sadly, he urged Carson that death lurked on the horizon.

"Carson, you shouldn't have come here. I tried to prevent you from coming to this place. There isn't a way out of this. The spirits have tricked you, played you for a fool. I tried to warn you, I tried to protect your children, but you didn't listen. You blocked me out with drugs, sex, and alcohol."

Stuck between worlds, Carson detached from his human form, floating in the aether. There, but not there. Nowhere and everywhere.

"Carson, my boy, not only have you killed yourself, but you've endangered your brother, his girlfriend, and their unborn baby. I didn't remember until after I crossed over, but this is a bad place. You never should have come back. Look what it's cost you."

"I didn't mean to. I was hurt and lost, mourning you and my innocence. I don't have a family like Brennan does. No one wants me. I'm a wreck, and all I wanted was acceptance—to discover my heritage, and where it is I come from. Now I'm ashamed and full of regret; it's cost me my life and so much more. If Brennan did not play me, then I hope he can be spared."

"You don't understand, my grandchild, this is prophecy. This is inevitable. If it wasn't this year, it may be the next or so on. Liquid and bone remind you of home. That's where this treachery starts."

"I don't understand," Carson's new form stated. "What treachery?"

"Your grandmother. She's evil, and she's cursed us all. She stole me from my life, and stole you from yours. We never stood a chance. Do you know what it's like to know that those connected to you tarnished your existence? That everything you've ever known was diseased and malnourished because you come from darkness. True darkness, too—not some glorious, celestial body of wonder. No, sir, this darkness is inherently bad and wants to ruin your soul for eternity. It doesn't stop there; it continues into your next life, into your next cycle of birth and death. It's terrifying, a true succubus."

Carson listened, then the chrysalis met the moonlight.

CHAPTER 25

BRENNAN FROZE, COMPREHENSION FILLING his brain. Brianna wasn't human, and she delighted in the suffering of others. Fiona lowered her shirt and began driving again in silence. Her face was hard to read, and Brennan was still processing what she showed him.

"How did she do that to you?"

Fiona chuckled dryly. "Brianna forms herself into a beautiful woman, doesn't she?"

Brennan agreed mentally, then felt shame thinking of his girlfriend and unborn child back home. "I guess so."

"We met at the bar one night. I had recently come to grips with who I was, and like clockwork, this gorgeous redhead appeared at the end of the bar. She was making eyes at me, and I was lonely. We started chatting, and she made it clear she wanted to go home with me. I was beside myself with my good luck."

Brennan thought about how forceful Brianna was that night with him and understood. They weren't sexual partners; they were prey. It made him wonder if Carson had gotten caught in her web and how he made it out.

Fiona went on. "We went back to my place, and long story short, it was amazing. However, I woke up later that night with Brianna on top of me. Not in a good way. She had me pinned down with her hands, except they were more like talons, and her strength was insane. I couldn't move or scream. She had some sort of power over me. Her face had changed, too. It was awful, truly terrifying. She was trying to consume me."

"Jesus," Brennan muttered.

"I struggled to get her off me and finally was able to get to the edge of the bed and pull myself to the floor. She was livid, her mouth opened wider than it should have, and she roared. I got up and ran, but she caught up with me at the door. I almost made it out when she lashed out at me, tearing open my stomach."

Brennan stared in amazement, feeling like there was no way it could be true... but he'd seen the scars. "How did you get away? Survive?"

Fiona turned off the main road onto a dirt road, which appeared to disappear into nothingness. "Dreadful."

"The cat?"

Fiona turned on her lights as the sky seemed to darken. "Yes. She came sauntering up the stairs to my bedroom, and Brianna froze. By Brianna, I mean the creepy creature she'd become. She backed away, making a guttural growl, and Dreadful pounced toward her. Brianna screamed, then bolted for the open window. She crawled out of the window and disappeared into the night."

"Because of a cat? Are Sidhe scared of cats?" Brennan asked, confused.

Fiona shrugged. "Your guess is as good as mine. I can say Brianna was afraid of Dreadful, but I don't know if that's a Sidhe thing. Not willing to test the theory again."

Brennan didn't know if she was joking or being serious and kept his face straight. "Where are we?"

"Word has it, this is where Flynn's place is. I don't know the exact location, but this is the general area. I figured we'd drive around and see if we can spot it, yeah?"

"What are we looking for? A house?"

"I suppose."

Brennan shook his head, peering out into the countryside. "Well, that narrows it down, doesn't it?"

Fiona laughed. "I don't think they put signs out front announcing they live there."

"I guess not. So how will we know?"

"I really don't have a clue, but this is all we have to go off of, isn't it? Let's hope something makes sense."

Brennan was overcome with a wave of gratitude for Fiona taking the time to help him search for Carson. He owed her big time. They wound through back roads, occasionally passing a house here and there. Most, they were able to rule out simply because people were outside or the house clearly had children living there. Finally, they came to a fork in the road, each fork having a house down it off in the distance. Fiona let the car idle as she considered which way to go from there.

A feeling came over Brennan, and he knew which was the right way to go. “Left.”

Fiona eyed him, then bobbed her head, turning the car down the left fork. “Twin thing again?”

Brennan chuckled. “I think so.”

They headed down the road toward the house, which appeared abandoned. Brennan swore he could feel Carson’s presence around him. Was that a good sign? Nearing the house, Fiona slowed the car and scanned around the area. An old car was in the driveway, but otherwise the house appeared empty.

Fiona eased behind the other car and glanced at Brennan. “Now what?”

“Let me go knock on the door. No one knows me. I’ll say we got turned around and are looking for directions if anyone answers. Do you have sunglasses you can put on so you might not be recognizable?”

Fiona dug in the glove box and pulled out a large pair of sunglasses, slipping them on. Brennan could see his reflection in the lenses and realized how haggard he looked. He opened the door. “I’ll be right back.”

He jogged up to the front door, not convinced they were at the right house, considering at the state of it. The roof was practically falling in. He raised his hand and knocked, surprised when the door swung up on its own. He waited a second, then peered in. "Hello? Anyone home?"

The house remained silent, and he stepped through the doorway, watching his feet in case the floor was rotten. "I'm lost. Looking for directions. Anyone here?"

Again, nothing. He wandered in, glancing around. The home had once been occupied, as there was furniture and other signs of life in there, but he guessed it was only squatters. Nothing about it said anyone treated it like a home.

Hands grabbed him from behind, and he gasped. "Sorry, I was lost! I wasn't sure anyone lived here," he explained as he whipped around.

Fiona was staring at him with a grin on her face as she pulled off her sunglasses. "Didn't mean to startle you. I saw you go inside and thought it was safe to come in."

"Geez, Fiona, I think I just tasted my heart in my throat. I don't think anyone lives here."

She glanced around. "This is the place."

"How do you know?"

"I just do. It doesn't look like someone lives here. But someone does. Flynn only needs a place to bring people to, not to live, if that makes sense."

Brennan sort of did. If Flynn wasn't human, he didn't need a human house. However, if he was luring prey, he needed to keep up appearances to get them under his control. "Let's look around. I need to see if I can find any clues about Carson being here or where he went."

They began in the living room and moved to the kitchen. Someone had been there, as there were glasses on the counter, not covered in dust. Room by room, they looked, not finding anything. An odd object on the wall caught Brennan's eye, and he moved closer. It was a circle woven of reeds and bones. He touched it and shook his head.

"My grandmother has this exact wall hanging," he murmured, wondering if it was an Irish thing.

Fiona came over to look, and her eyes grew wide as she turned to face him. "She does?"

"Yeah, is this like a traditional Irish wall hanging?" Brennan asked, peering closer. The bones almost looked human, not that he was an expert on bones.

"No."

Brennan glanced at Fionna, who had taken a step back. "What is it?"

"You know how you hear about Fairy Circles?"

"You mean like mushrooms and shit in the woods you aren't supposed to step into?"

Fiona nodded. "Yeah. This is like that. Story has it that the Sidhe hang these when they are out of their element for protection from outsiders."

Brennan frowned and reached out to touch the hanging. "My grandmother has this."

Fiona met his eyes, hers worried. "Your grandmother without a last name?"

He nodded as comprehension washed over him. "Shit. Are you saying my grandmother is Sidhe?"

"I'm not saying anything. You are. I am telling you what this is, and you are saying your grandmother has one. What do you think?"

The room began spinning, and Brennan stepped back to sit on a dilapidated couch, his head in his hands. If his grandmother were Sidhe, that would explain so much about everything. About her cruelty, about his mother and sister's deaths. No, murders. About the weird visits he'd had his whole life. About Carson spiraling out of control. About his strange fetishes.

It meant they were part Sidhe, too.

A glimmer of something by the coffee table caught Brennan's eye. He reached down and scooped it up, his heart skipping a beat. A thick chain bracelet with the letter *C* sat in his hand, and he ran his fingers over it, then over a matching one with the letter *B* on his own wrist.

"What is it?" Fiona asked, coming closer.

"This is Carson's."

"How do you know?"

Brennan held his wrist up. "Our grandfather gave these to us on our eighteenth birthday. We never take them off in honor of our grandfather. Something must have happened for Carson to lose it at this house."

Fiona sat beside him. "So Carson was here?"

Brennan nodded, slipping the bracelet into his pocket. "He was, I know for sure."

The question remained:

Where was Carson now?

CHAPTER 26

PULSATING, ILLUMINATING AN IRIDESCENT green, the chrysalis hovered above the bog. Translucent, yet vibrant, oozing a sludgy slime. The gunk from the bottom of the bog bed seeped from the white threads, glistening in the night. Hypnotic but eerie, Carson lay partially visible inside. All anyone could make out if they stumbled upon the chrysalis floating atop the water was a person trapped inside, hidden in the blueish hue of Carson's coccoon.

This tight space is wearing on me. I need out. I need to be free. I'm a full person now. When does this metamorphosis end? I feel everything; my nerves are tingling, my skin burning. The fire in me continued to rage, despite the changes brewing. This damn thing is going to become a coffin if I can't get out. This is my tombstone, and I'm dying inside it. When someone finds me in a week, I'll be skin and bones, melting in the spring sun.

The voices are surrounding me, and they scare me. They want me dead, to die in this cocoon, or whatever it is. Chrysalis, they call it, but I don't really know anymore. None of this seems real; all of it is far too fantastical for me. My skin is pale, and my body feels different.

Who am I?

The forest brooded with inky sprites stretching across the terrain. Flynn led the way, allowing their dark energy to encompass the entirety of the bog, essentially making it a death trap. Even if Carson crawled out, the Sidhe would latch onto him and pull him under. The only thing Carson could do was wait and hope death wasn't near. What he didn't know, is he wasn't their mark. Not who they wanted. He was simply bait. A toy to play with once they got what they were seeking.

You won't make it through this. This is your own doing. You deserve this. You had the bright idea to come to Ireland to get closer to Grandad, and here you are trapped in a strange form, unsure what's real anymore. What on Earth did you get yourself into? Listen to Grandpa, the family is cursed, and there is no way to break it. Maybe my death will end it? Maybe I am the key? Otherwise, my entire family may suffer. Maybe all I can do now is accept death and welcome it. My life's been wasted. I partied, slept around, and never grew up. Let Brennan's baby girl enter this world, let her spirit walk the earth, and let mine wither away. It's time.

I greet the reaper.

Laughing, the evil spirits gatekeeping the bog prepared for their sacrifice. "Kill the baby and the mother," Carson heard a spirit say. "It's time."

"Please, don't hurt them. Take me, let my niece and Marly be. Let them live. Take me. I'm a drug addict, a drunk, and I left my brother and family to get played by a bunch of tricksters. I don't know anymore, maybe the acid pushed me over the edge. I'm not sure what to believe anymore," Carson argued, yelling at the Sidhe surrounding the lone O'Leary. "Take me!"

The dark entities appeared around the bog, making their presence known. With their eyes on the chrysalis, they sang, ready to make a sacrifice. "One two, what will Carson do?"

The bed was connected to Marly and the baby, much like an umbilical cord. A long, plasmatic rope ran from the very bottom of the bog to the mother and daughter in the States. The bizarre, jet black cable looked like a rotting thread, dripping with bioluminescence, and years of decay.

Back home, Marly could feel the imaginary umbilical cord sucking the life out of her and the baby. Concerned, she put her hand over her belly, feeling the horrors of the bog swirling inside her.

Worried, Carson pressed on the inside of the chrysalis. "Help me!"

It was of no use.

THE CORD CONNECTED TO Marly fed off her baby, depleting her small body. The Sidhe huddled around Carson, enjoying his misery, and knew the unborn little girl would be theirs, joining their family of evil spirits as their own.

The O'Leary family never stood a chance. Carson broke the barrier, and now death drew closer.

Across the Atlantic, Marly left her mother's house and sat back at the apartment she shared with Brennan, hoping to hear from him soon. Wishing he would come home. A knock at her door pulled her from bed. She stumbled down the hall, weak and disoriented. "Who would be banging on my door at this hour?"

Looking out the window, she saw a handsome young man smiling at her. He was warm and inviting and instantly made Marly comfortable. She no longer had control over her own decisions, the man at the door manipulating her mind as she answered the door.

"Can I help you?" she asked, gazing at the handsome fellow peering back at her. His eyes were calm and inviting like the blue of the sea. They changed to green, then brown and blue again, before fading to black. Marly was entranced, patting her belly as she smiled in the delusion.

Flynn grinned back at her, knowing he had her under his spell. Much like Carson, Marly sat ready to jump at his every beck and call.

"Marly, right? I'm an old friend of Brennan and Carson's from school. Brennan called me from Ireland and told me to stop by and check on you, to see how you were feeling. My name's Flynn. May I come in?" Flynn asked, mimicking an American accent flawlessly.

Marly was hypnotized, falling into Flynn's dreamy stare. She'd do whatever he asked, completely under his mind control. In fact, he wasn't even standing there, every bit of him a figment of her imagination. If her neighbors saw her, they'd see a woman talking to nobody, rubbing her belly, and smirking into nothing.

"Sure," she said, letting him in. "I'm feeling fine, thank you."

"You have a lovely home," Flynn said. "When's the baby due?"

"Thanks, in a few months."

Flynn's face turned, and a sly, evil smirk stretched across his face. "Perfect."

CHAPTER 27

KNOWING CARSON WAS NO longer at the house, Fiona and Brennan stepped outside and wandered around the property, looking for anything that might let them know where he'd gone. A figure appeared across the wide open field between the bog and the house.

At first, it was hard to tell if it was a man or a woman, but Brennan knew for sure it wasn't Carson. He'd know his brother's gait and outline anywhere. As the figure grew closer, Brennan could make out that it was a woman.

However, not just any woman.

Brianna.

She was walking right toward them, and Brennan felt Fiona stiffen beside him. Brianna moved at an unusually quick pace, approaching them as if she were gliding. Brennan glanced at Fiona, who had her eyes locked on Brianna.

He understood her trepidation. Brianna tried to kill her. Possibly even killed Carson.

"I'm okay. You can go," he whispered to Fiona, not wanting her to be harmed again.

She shook her head. "You have no way back to town. Besides, she doesn't get to scare me that easily."

"Did you ever call the police on her?"

"No. I knew there was no point. If I told them some woman I took home turned into a creature and attacked me, they'd be more likely to lock me up than her."

That was a fair point. Brianna was now visible, and she had a wide, wicked grin on her face. A face that seemed to morph within seconds. Brennan swallowed his fear and stood his ground.

"What do you want?" he asked her.

Brianna laughed coldly as she moved on them like a predator. "Question is, what do you want? Because I bet we have it."

We? Brennan did a quick scan around, but it appeared like Brianna was alone. What did she mean by what she said? Was she in cahoots with the guy Flynn? "Did you do something to my brother?"

"That sweet little piece of meat who was ready to hump everything in sight?" Brianna asked.

She wasn't wrong, but Brennan didn't appreciate Brianna speaking about his brother like that. "Where is he? Did you and Flynn hurt him?"

This brought a snicker from her ruby lips, and she tipped her head, causing her red hair to cascade over one shoulder. "Define hurt. He sure can put up a fight, but all the drugs in his system made him super easy to manipulate."

Rage soared through Brennan, and he took a step toward Brianna. "You bitch! I swear if you did anything to hurt my brother, I'll kill you."

"Will you, then?" she asked with a smirk. "Don't get too sure of yourself, boy. You don't know who you are playing with. I'll tell you this. Your sibling is alive, but he is undergoing quite the transformation."

"What the fuck does that mean? What exactly are you?" Brennan spat.

Brianna winked at Fiona, who took a step back. "Oh, I think you already know the answer to that question. The real question is, what exactly are you?"

Unfortunately, Brennan suspected he also knew the answer to that question. His grandmother was Sidhe; he knew that now. How she ended up with his grandfather and in America was a whole other quandary. Brianna took another step toward him, batting her eyes with a fake air of innocence.

"Do you want to go see your brother?"

Brennan knew it was a trap, yet he couldn't stop himself from answering. He nodded and set his mouth. "Take me to him. He'd better be alright."

Fiona reached out and put her hand on his arm to stop him. "Don't trust her, Brennan. She'll say anything to get what she wants."

Brianna smiled and kept her eyes on Fiona. "Aw, dear, don't be so quick to judge. You were awfully open to me the night we fucked. You were by far the most fun I've had between the sheets as a human. You almost made me want to turn. We can't have that, though, can we? So, I figured if I took you out, there would be no temptation. You were quite the fighter. Turned me on to be honest."

Fiona shuddered and moved slightly behind Brennan. He glared at Brianna. "Enough of the fucking games. This is between you and me, so leave Fiona alone."

Brianna shrugged with disinterest. "Pity. I'd like a piece of that ass again."

Brennan was over her bullshit and ready to take charge. "Take me to my brother now."

Brianna licked her lips. "Watch for for out what you ask for. If I take you with me, there are some things you need to understand."

"Like what?"

"Like your grandmother was one of us, and she broke the rule. The covenant."

Brennan frowned. "How?"

Brianna delighted in dragging out the information and raised her perfect red eyebrows. "Old Deirdre stole a small human child when she was a youngling herself.

She brought him back to the bog to live with us. The elders wanted to kill him, but we have lived in peace with humans, and they didn't want to risk it."

"Peace with humans. Are you serious?" Fiona muttered incredulously.

"Darling, we could do so much worse to humans, trust me," Brianna retorted. "We may lure you in and take advantage of your weakness, but we rarely kill without reason."

She didn't say *never*, she said *rarely*. Brennan didn't want to get off track. "So what happened?"

"They didn't know who to return him to and couldn't let the humans know where we live, so they allowed Deirdre to keep him as a pet. Unfortunately, Deidre lost her senses and fell in love with the boy when they were both teenagers. They ran off together and did the unspeakable. They cross-bred."

Cross-bred.

Brennan's father was half-Sidhe and half-human. Then he had children with a human, as well, making Carson and Brennan a quarter Sidhe. Thinking of his poor mother and baby sibling, Brennan asked, "Why did they kill my mother and my sister?"

"Ah, you figured that out, did you? No females are allowed to breed with humans. Male children who come from this atrocity are protected by the covenant. In a way. Females are not. Because they breed, they must be killed.

Deirdre knew this. She broke the covenant and brought harm to our community."

Brennan took in everything she said and tried to let it absorb into his brain. "How did she bring harm to you?"

"Well, first your brother showed up here, now you. The draw of being Sidhe is too strong to stay away for long. You risk our community by bringing in outsiders and exposing where we live," Brianna said, her eyes locked on Fiona.

"Just give me my brother, then, and we will leave for good," Brennan bargained.

"What about your daughter?" Brianna asked knowingly. "Have you even considered her?"

They were going to kill his daughter. Per the covenant, she and Marly were to be sacrificed. Brennan felt his knees start to buckle, and Fiona supported him to keep him from falling on the ground. He imagined Marly and the baby back home, and terror washed over him. "You better not hurt them."

Brianna shrugged with a flip of her hand. "Oh, it's in the covenant. There's nothing I can do about it."

Fiona made a guttural, horrified sound in her throat. "You would kill a baby?"

"We've done it before. We'll never get Deirdre back, so a sacrifice needs to be made."

"You can't," Brennan pleaded. "They have nothing to do with this."

"Everyone has everything to do with everything," Brianna countered. "However, there might be something you can do to stop it."

"What? I'll do anything."

"Come with me."

Fiona went to protest, but Brennan met her eyes. "I have to, Fiona. They have control over everyone I love. I am nothing without my family. I need to go."

Fiona watched him, her eyes filled with pain. "You might not come back."

"I know, it's a risk I need to take. Go to Flynn's house and wait a bit. I'll come back if I get out of this. I have to find Carson and try to save my family."

Fiona nodded and glared at Brianna, her normally calm eyes filled with rage. "I hope you rot in hell."

Brianna chuckled. "We don't have hell. That's a human construct, but thanks, darling."

Fiona backed away, keeping her eyes on Brennan. He bobbed his head and gave her a small smile. "Thanks for your help. Don't forget me."

"I won't. Come back, you always have a place to stay with me," Fiona promised.

Brianna yawned. "Isn't that sweet? Now, let's get moving before it gets dark. You need to see this in the light."

See what? Brennan wondered. Brianna began the trek across the field to the bog, moving almost too fast for Brennan to keep up, even though he had longer legs than her. Fiona waited a few minutes before leaving, then disappeared out of sight. Brennan felt very, very alone.

They made it to the edge of the bog as the sun began to color the sky with beautiful hues of red and orange. Brennan glanced around, but it looked just like a bog. Was this some sort of trick? Had she lured Brennan out only to mess with him? Or harm him?

He could hear what sounded like whispers on the wind and peered closer, seeing shadows move around the bog. Something hanging right above the water caught his eye, and he tried to understand what he was looking at. It appeared to be some sort of large, iridescent cocoon, levitating in the air. Too big for an insect. Almost big enough for a human.

A *human.*

Eyes wide, he rotated to face Brianna, and she was staring at the structure with appreciation. "Isn't the chrysalis beautiful?"

Brennan didn't understand and looked back at the hovering structure. "What is it?"

"Not what. Who," Brianna replied proudly.

Who. She'd told him Carson was going through a transformation. Suspecting the answer, Brennan asked in horror, "Where's Carson?"

Brianna pointed at the chrysalis and smiled knowingly. "Welcome home."

Chapter 28

Brennan stared in horror at the giant chrysalis, finally understanding what was happening to his brother. "Carson is in there?"

Brianna raised an eyebrow. "Yes and no. Your brother went in, but your brother won't come out."

"What the hell does that mean?"

"You know when caterpillars form a cocoon around them to turn into butterflies?"

What the fuck was she talking about? "Is Carson in there or not?" Brennan yelled, frustrated with the endless games. He scanned the surface of the water for the quickest way to get to the cocoon.

"Carson is in there, but no longer resides in Carson's body," Brianna answered cryptically.

Brennan stared at the hovering chrysalis and began to sob. "What do you want with us? Why are you doing this?"

Brianna sighed, turning serious. "Many years ago, one of our own was taken from us. She started the process, but your grandfather finished it by taking her away from us."

"I don't understand. You said she kidnapped him. How is this his fault? How is this my fault or Carson's?"

Brianna laughed, drawing Brennan's attention to her. She shifted, and what he saw standing in front of him was like nothing he'd ever seen. What he thought was her turning into an old woman on the street wasn't exactly right.

Yes, she appeared old, but now he could see it wasn't human. Her arms hung low and her shoulders slightly hunched, supporting a large, bulbous head on almost no neck. Her body shrank and became withered. Standing before him was a creature of sorts.

"What the hell?"

Brianna reached out and touched his cheek with her long, gnarled finger. "This is what we look like when we aren't presenting for your comfort. This is what your grandmother looked like before she presented to trap your grandfather. Had he seen this, he would have run away. Instead, he fell in love with her human shell."

Brennan frowned and tipped his head. "If that's true, why doesn't my father look like you? Why don't Carson and I appear that way?"

"You couldn't if you tried. You have too much human blood in you. Your father chooses not to, as does your grandmother. Do you ever feel like you aren't human? Do you crave things you feel you shouldn't?"

Brennan wiped the tears off his face and nodded. "I have odd fetishes. Carson is an addict. I see things. Faces when I try to sleep. Monsters."

"Like this?" Brianna asked, and let her face morph into what he saw when he closed his eyes when he went to bed since he was a child.

"You have been stalking me?"

"Stalking, watching, waiting. We knew you would eventually come home."

"I can't stay here. I have a fiancé, a child on the way. I need to go back to them," Brennan insisted, feeling guilty for leaving Marly alone.

"If you go back to them, they will die."

"What do you mean?"

"You crossed the line. Like your father and grandmother before you. Your father was allowed to live because he was male, as were you and Carson. No females who mate with the Sidhe are permitted to survive. No female children born of that abomination may live. Your woman and daughter will be slaughtered," Brianna explained as if she were reading off a recipe.

Brennan fell to his knees, crying out. "Take my grandmother back, let us be free of all this."

"It's too late. Once your grandmother bred with a human and had a child, she tainted herself. She is not welcome back. A sacrifice must be made." Brianna pointed at the chrysalis. "Your brother belongs to us now."

Brennan's eyes followed her outstretched hand, and he saw the chrysalis throb and glow under the moonlight. "What can I do to stop this? How can I save Marly and my child?"

Brianna flicked her finger in the air and turned to face him. "You must break the curse."

"How do I do that?" Brennan begged. "Tell me!"

"You are the firstborn son. Your father was the firstborn son of your grandmother's, but he was willing to sacrifice his daughter and wife to stay in the human world."

"He knew? That's why he and my grandmother killed them? My mother and sister were innocent!"

"Yes, a sacrifice must be made. One of ours is waiting near your woman and unborn child, waiting on the word to remove them from existence," Brianna answered.

Marly. Sweet, loving Marly. Brennan's heart broke for all the times he let her down, for not protecting her from all of this. She had no idea who he really was, yet would still pay the price for it. He shook his head.

"You said my father sacrificed my mother and sister. I am not doing that. Why would they need to die?"

Brianna grinned, her strangely wide mouth stretching across her leathery face. "As I said, a sacrifice must be made."

"What if I stay here as the sacrifice? Take me instead of them," Brennan offered, thinking Brianna would brush him off.

She turned her head, her eyes surprised. "You would give up your human life, your woman, your child, to return to your destiny?"

"If you will let them live, I will do anything. Nothing matters more to me than their lives. I am nothing without them," Brennan promised.

"You will burn."

Burn? What did she mean? "I don't understand?"

"You must be reduced to nothing to break the curse. You will become ash," Brianna answered.

"I will die?"

"Yes."

Brennan placed his face in his hands. "What about Carson?"

Brianna glanced at the cocoon and grimaced, knowing there was no other way. "Carson is no more."

"He's dead?"

"Death is only a transformation. Carson is no longer your brother."

Brennan frowned, tired of the cryptic messages. "Is Carson in there?"

"Yes."

"If I stay, can my brother come out?"

"No."

"What are you saying? What is happening to Carson in there?" Brennan asked, trying to make sense of what was happening.

"Carson is nothing more than the liquid of the cosmos, like the caterpillar."

Caterpillar. "A caterpillar becomes a butterfly; it doesn't die in the cocoon. It forms into something else," Brennan countered.

"Now you're getting it," Brianna answered.

Carson was transforming. Into what? Brennan took a shuddering breath and stared at the pulsing chrysalis, his mind racing. Carson was no longer his *brother*, Brianna said. He wasn't asking the right questions. Carson was alive and transforming.

"If I stay, will you set Carson free and leave Marly and my daughter alone?"

Brianna tipped her head, considering. "You will suffer greatly. You will wish for death."

"I will suffer to save them. To end this all. Will my daughter be safe for the rest of her life?"

"Yes, as long as she never comes here. Are you willing to take Carson's place?"

"In the chrysalis?"

"No, that was his destiny; your's is in the flames," Brianna answered, her eyes focused on him.

Brennan nodded, knowing there was no other way. "Yes. I will take his place."

Brianna waved her fingers in the air, and the chrysalis began to descend back toward the bog. The glow increased, and the pod began to flicker with multicolored lights as the throbbing increased. Brennan could make out what appeared to be an embryo inside the flesh-like covering.

The chrysalis sank into the bog, and bubbles rose in its descent. It disappeared, and the bog went dark. Brennan jumped to his feet, his eyes scanning the surface. “You said you would set him free!”

“Shhhh,” Brianna replied impatiently, her wrinkled face focused on the surface of the water. “The metamorphosis is not complete.”

Not understanding, Brennan went to the edge of the bog, gazing down. The water began to ripple as something came to the surface. Not the chrysalis, a person. Brennan stepped back as the body floated to the surface and began to twitch. It wasn’t his brother.

A woman stumbled out of the water toward him, naked and shaking. Brennan pulled his jacket off and ran to her, wrapping her in his coat. She fell to her knees and coughed, water coming out of her mouth. She gazed up at Brennan, her eyes confused.

“Brennan?”

Brennan took a step back. How did she know who he was? “How do you know my name?”

The woman looked down at her body and stood up, moving parts of her anatomy as she stared in disbelief.

She peered at Brennan, and he felt something stir in him. Recognition. She stepped closer, and he saw something in her eyes. She reached up and touched his face.

"Brennan, it's me. Carson."

Brennan jerked back and glared at Brianna. "What's the meaning of this? Is this a trick?"

Brianna began to cackle. "No trick, boy. You offered to trade places. Carson is who she was always meant to be. It's time to go. You must come with me, and Carson must leave before she is taken back into the bog."

Brennan stared at Carson, his mind reeling. As crazy as it was to see his sibling in this form, it now made total sense. Carson was never meant to be his brother. All of his running and addiction were Carson struggling with not knowing who he was. Brennan could see it on Carson's face. An understanding. He stepped forward and wrapped his sister in his arms. Carson hugged him tightly. They had finally made it back to each other, only to be ripped apart again.

For good.

"I need you to do something for me, Carson," Brennan whispered between his tears.

Carson stepped back and nodded. "Of course. Anything, Bren."

"I am staying here. It was the only way to save you, Marly, and my daughter. Grandma cursed all of us. I need you to go back and let Marly know how much I love her.

Let her know I didn't want to leave her. I need you to watch over my daughter. She, nor Marly, can never come here. Make sure she knows me, okay?"

Carson let tears slide down her cheeks as she took Brennan's hand. "I need you, Brennan. I can't go back alone. You're all I have left."

"You have to. I made a deal to set you free. To save my family. To save you. Marly and the baby are everything to me, as are you. I'm sorry I wasn't there for you before. I love you, Carson."

"It's time," Brianna said, growing impatient.

"Fuck you," Brennan replied as he faced the sibling he'd never given enough credit to. He leaned forward and kissed Carson's cheek. "You are beautiful."

Carson smiled through pained eyes. "I will miss you, Brennan. They can't take you away from me. I will protect your daughter with my life and tell her all about her brave father. What should I tell her? Who should I say I am?"

"Tell Marly you're my sister, now. She'll understand. Marly has a big heart and an open mind. You can't tell her about any of this, though. That's part of the deal. Tell her... tell her I was in a freak accident and died, but that I love her and the baby more than life itself."

They embraced, and Brennan turned to leave. He stopped and faced Carson. "One more thing. I need you to find someone when you get home. She will help you with

your change. She has been my friend and confidante, and I trust her more than anything."

"How will I find her?"

"Go down to the waterfront. She does business there."

"What's her name?"

"Desiree. Tell her Brennan sent you."

Carson bobbed her head and smiled through tears. "I love you, Brennan."

"I love you, Carson. Go. You know where Flynn's house is. There is a woman there named Fiona. Tell her who you are, and she'll get you back to town. Never forget me."

"Never."

They hugged one last time, and Carson headed toward the house, shivering in the cold. She drew Brennan's coat around her as she used the moon to light the way. She glanced back and saw Brennan disappear into the murky water. As she ran across the field, she heard his screams of pain lift into the night and knew he was burning beneath the bog.

Chapter 29

Back in the States, Carson wasn't sure what to think or what to feel. Flashes of being in the womb as a baby plagued her, and she felt spirits around her. She could see evil entities overtaking their mother's belly, manipulating and digging into every part of her anatomy, Carson, and Brennan. Being in utero ached, a torturous experience.

Recalling her life as male, she remembered the dark spirits changing her, making sure their desire took shape.

Staring in the mirror, she admired her new body. It all made sense: the inward struggle, the disconnection to the old Carson, their grandmother's troubling presence, and their grandfather's death.

Inside, Carson missed Brennan deeply. The sorrow she felt for her grandfather flourished tenfold for Brennan. After all, he made the ultimate sacrifice, his soul for his loved ones' lives. Being in the chrysalis, although terrifying, Carson hoped her brother wasn't suffering as she had. The melting, the burning of flesh, the darkness, and the release—too much to bear.

"I need to tell Marly, bless her. She's going to be crushed. It's better than being dead and losing your unborn child, I guess. Damn it, why is my family so fucked up? I'll do everything I can, Brennan, I will. I promise."

Gazing at herself in the mirror, Carson felt something in the corner of the room. A shadow stretched across the wall, obsidian and intrusive—goosebumps forming on her arms. Glancing back at the mirror, she saw Brianna's reflection, the real her, too, the one with the crooked limbs and hunched back. Brianna's decrepit form shifted, and she smiled, revealing rotten, sharp teeth. Her gnarled flesh sagged off her bones as she seethed, "Hello, Carson."

Lurching forward, naked and bruised, Brianna's veins showed through her translucent skin as she made her way closer to Carson.

"Go away!" Panicking, Carson blinked, and Brianna vanished into thin air. "It's in you're head. They can't touch you over here."

She knew what she had to do. Before she spoke with Desiree or Marly, Carson had things to sort out, and fast. Searching through the phone book, she found the address she was looking for. She gathered her things and took a taxi to the nursing home. None of this would end until the person who started it no longer existed. Carson waited until the front desk was empty for a moment, snagged a pass from behind the counter, checked the residents' room numbers, and made her way down the hall to her grandmother's room.

Easing the door open, she could hear the television softly in the background. Her grandmother was sleeping in the bed, her head turned to one side away from the door. Carson crept in and went to her grandmother's bedside.

"Wake up, you old bitch."

The grandmother's eyes fluttered, and she turned her head toward Carson, recognizing her immediately. A flash of understanding crossed the old woman's face, and she sighed with disgust.

"That stupid boy sacrificed himself for you, didn't he? What an idiot."

Carson cringed. "Don't speak about Brennan that way. He undid what you did to all of us. I hate you."

Her grandmother cackled. "I see they had their way with you. Should have killed you, too. Both you children are worthless. You always were."

Carson didn't even have time to comprehend what she was doing as she found herself pressing a pillow over the old woman's face. Her grandmother struggled for a moment, then her body twisted into its original form as the life left her body. Carson pulled the pillow away and gasped at the sight. The hideous being left on the bed was terrifying in its original intended state.

Carson rushed out of the room and through an emergency exit as the monitors went off in her grandmother's room. Even if they caught her on camera, no one would know who she was. After all, the family had no girls, right?

Hurrying down the sidewalk, Carson didn't see where she was going when she ran headlong into another person. Going to apologize, she jerked back when she saw who it was. Flynn.

He grinned with one raised eyebrow. "Why, hello again, Carson. You are looking good."

Carson panicked, realizing he could only be in the States for one reason. "Marly?"

Flynn shrugged. "She's fine. A deal's a deal. I just wanted to see you again, that's all. You look good."

Carson watched as Flynn sauntered away. She considered going to find Marly to check on her. However, there was no reason for Flynn to lie. They got what they wanted. She stood on the sidewalk, unsure of what to do. She'd find Marly, but first, she needed to find someone else.

After walking the area of town down by the water, Carson was able to get information on who she was looking for. She followed the directions and found a door leading to a narrow set of stairs. She went up them and came to another door. Knocking three times, she tried to decide what she needed to say. It all sounded so unbelievable. No one would understand what happened to her and Brennan.

No one. The door swung open, and a beautiful woman answered.

Carson frowned and hoped she was at the right place. "Desiree?"

"In the flesh, honey," the woman replied.

A woman like her, Carson realized.

"I was told to find you. My brother... my brother, Brennan said you could help me," Carson sputtered out as tears slid down her cheek.

"Oh, darling, don't cry. Your brother?" Desiree eyed her up and down, seeming to understand without being told. "You must be Carson."

Carson nodded and burst into tears. Desiree led her inside to a small couch and patted her cheek as she sat down. Carson met her eyes. "I hate to tell you this. Brennan... he's dead."

Desiree searched Carson's face for truth as her eyes clouded with sadness. "I'm sorry, honey. He was something special. A tortured soul, but a good soul, nonetheless. He sent you to me?"

"Yes, he said you could help me with my..." Carson couldn't find the words. She was simply lost.

Desiree smiled and drew Carson in with her arms. "Your metamorphosis, darling."

"You know?"

"Us butterflies know how to bring each other home. You have me now, Carson. You aren't alone anymore."

For the first time in her life, Carson was whole.

The two women talked, honoring Brennan as the night went on. Desiree glanced at Carson and chose her words carefully.

"What really happened over there? Tell me. I felt something the last time I saw him. I saw things. Dark spirits around him. What really went on in Ireland? You can tell me, I promise."

Carson shook her head. "I can't. You won't believe me."

"Try me."

"Fine."

Carson went through it all, hashing out all the details, body horror, and all. The liquid. The heat.

"That is powerful, and I'm not surprised. Brennan was brave and genuine. He really loved you."

The words hit Carson like a ton of bricks. It was true, her brother loved her. It had only been the bog spirits playing tricks on them, ruining their lives from across the pond.

THE NEXT MORNING, CARSON knew she needed to head to Marly's. It would be difficult, but it needed to be done. Carson had a newfound appreciation for Marly. What she'd been through and who she was. What she meant to Brennan.

Arriving at Brennan and Marly's apartment, Carson wiped the tears from her face. She froze for a moment before she knocked, and within seconds, Marly was standing there looking at her. At first, Carson could tell Marly didn't recognize her. How could she? Before she could speak to explain, Marly knew.

"Carson?" Marly said, her words soft and inviting

"Yeah."

"Where's Brennan?"

"We need to talk. Can I come in?" Carson asked, fighting back tears.

Marly's face twisted, and her eyes widened with worry as Carson's words sunk in. "Of course. Where's Brennan? What happened, Carson?"

"I don't know how to tell you this, Marly, but Brennan isn't coming home."

"What do you mean?"

Carson knew the best thing to do was lie. Marly would never believe her, especially with Carson's history. "There was an accident in Ireland. I'm so sorry, Marly. Brennan drowned. His body wasn't recoverable. He sank into a deep crevice at the bottom of a pond."

Marly was shocked. "I don't understand. How did he drown in a pond? Brennan is a good swimmer."

"It was much bigger and deeper than you think. He was trying to save me, Marly. I'm really sorry. It's all my fault."

Grief hit her, and Marly collapsed, feeling her baby girl kicking inside her. "He was supposed to be a father. What do I tell Brianna?"

Carson winced. "Brianna?"

"Yeah, that's what I decided to name our baby girl."

"You can't. Don't, please. Don't name her that. Anything but that," Carson begged.

"Why, Carson? What's wrong with the name? What's going on?"

"Look, please pick another name. It's all I ask. That name has some bad history with our family. It's cursed."

Marly stared at Brennan's twin, unsure what to think, noticing the honesty in Carson's eyes and nodded. "Alright, I trust you. I won't name the baby Brianna."

Carson spent the day comforting Marly as she made memorial arrangements. Even without a body, they were having a service. An Irish funeral of sorts. They were honoring Brennan, cherishing the man Marly never got a chance to marry, but was always part of them because he loved her and the baby more than his own life. Even if Brennan's corpse was nowhere to be found, they were having a ceremony, and honoring Brennan O'Leary for the sacrifices he made for all of them.

Brennan would live on in his daughter's life. The life he made sure she got to live.

Even when it cost him his own.

Epilogue

Baby Brigid was six months old and crawling like a caterpillar across the carpet. Her movements made Carson uneasy, reminding her of her time in the bog. However, she looked past the darkness and saw the light in her beautiful, happy niece.

Brigid was a beacon.

"Brennan would be so proud of you. Your daddy loves you, little one. I'm sorry he couldn't be here. He watches over you, Brigid, forever. You have a mommy who loves you very much and an aunt who will always be there for you. No matter what."

Marly watched her child and smiled. "She's beautiful, isn't she? She has her father's eyes."

"She does," Carson replied. "She's so pure and innocent. I'm glad she's here. It makes me feel like part of Brennan is, too."

"I wish he were here to see this. How am I going to tell Brigid when she's old enough that her daddy isn't here? What do I say?"

"You tell her, her father was a hero. A brave soul who died for his family."

Marly nodded and smiled as she watched Brigid skirt across the floor in an army crawl. "Thanks, Carson."

"Listen, I have something for you...well, for Brigid. It was Brennan's," Carson said, retrieving the jewelry from her bag.

Carson handed Marly the chain bracelet, her eyes catching the *B* engraved on it.

"How do you have this?" she asked, running her fingers over the letter.

"I tried to save him, Marly. I really did. It slipped off his wrist. It's all that's left of him. I think Brigid should have it."

"Oh, Carson. Thank you so much. I know she will cherish it as she gets older. I love you."

"I love you, too."

They hugged and let go, eyeing Brigid as she wiggled across the floor. The infant smiled as she spied a funny little creature in the corner of the room. Reaching out, the baby clawed at the air, extending her fingers toward the small being stirring out of sight of the adults. Something only she could see.

Her face twisted in frustration, then baby Brigid began to cry. Something was taunting her. Luring the child from a destiny she couldn't escape...

Calling.

Calling across the ocean.

Calling from Ireland.

Calling from the ancient forest.

Calling from beneath the bog.

Acknowledgements

A BIG thank you to our readers and everyone who has supported us this year... you remind us what we are doing matters.

Thank you to our ARC and Beta readers for providing feedback!

For all the ancestors who crossed the ocean for a better life, and for those who went back.

About the Authors

D.Z. Hollow and Juliet Rose are husband and wife authors living in the North Georgia mountains with a slew of rescue animals. Through their shared Irish ancestry they created this story. You can read more of their work by going to abovetheraincollective.com

ALSO BY JULIET & D.Z.

Collaboration:

Attack of the Trees

D.Z. Hollow:

Cartecay

Broken Window

Glob Bunny

Mirror Island (as Justin Sexton)

The Nomad (as Justin Sexton)

Juliet Rose:

Do Over

We Don't Matter

Prick of the Needle

Through the Surface

Trigger Point

Catch the Earth

Carrying the Dead

Stitched Together

In Dreams, We Fly

By the Dimming Light

Expectation of Pain

Done.

Unquiet Forest

Soul Umbra

www.ingramcontent.com/pod-product-compliance
Lightning Source LLC
LaVergne TN
LVHW100526110826
845146LV00002B/787

* 9 7 9 8 9 9 3 3 7 1 7 2 6 *